PROTECTING JOSIE

PROTECTING JOSIE

A NOVEL

KATIE O'CONNOR

SNARKY HEART PRESS

Published April 2019 by Snarky Heart Press and Katie O'Connor (katieohwrites.com)

ISBN: 978-1-9990192-3-5 (Print Edition)
ISBN: 978-1-9990192-4-2 (Kindle Edition)
ISBN: 978-1-9990192-2-8 (Other Digital Editions)

Design and cover art by Jenna Howard.
Copyediting by FireChicken Press, LLC.
Formatting by Shelley Kassian.

*This one is for Linda Brown.
For your love, affection and unwavering support.*

ACKNOWLEDGMENTS

Despite the endless hours I spend sitting alone at my computer, I'm never really alone. I have a large circle of local and internet author friends who always have my back. As always, they keep me sane. They prop me up when I'm riddled with doubt. They smooth my plot holes, provide encouragement, and keep me rational when life goes astray. Their backup is invaluable. For this reason and so many others, I dedicate this book to Shelley Kassian, Jenn Howard, Kara Leigh Miller, M.K. Stelmack, Brenda Sinclair, and A.M. Westerling. Thank you, ladies, for keeping me strong and positive.

Thanks to Fire Chicken Press for the great editing and to Jenna Howard for the lovely cover.

CHAPTER 1

*J*uggling a box of miscellaneous pieces from her past, Josie Lyons fumbled in her purse, searching for her car keys. Why hadn't she found them before leaving the library for the last time? This sandstone and slate building had been her life for years. She'd grown up coming here several times a week for new reading material. After graduating from university with her Master's of Library Science degree, she'd lucked out and gotten hired in her home town. Now, she'd been fired.

Fired!

She could barely believe it. She rarely took vacation or sick days. She'd only been late once since starting. Her boss, Ramone Garcia, had laid her off, claiming cutbacks, which was a blatant lie. She wasn't an idiot, and she was—or rather she had been—on the library board of directors. His cutback claim didn't make sense. Their small-town library had just received a two-million-dollar grant from an anonymous donor. Two million would run the library for nearly a decade, if not longer. Garcia was lying, plain and simple. What she couldn't fathom was why.

Ideally, she'd have liked to tell Ramone she'd never step foot in the building again after he fired her without cause, and she'd nearly bit through her tongue to keep from doing so. But the fact was, Josie was a died-in-the-wool bibliophile. Books were her passion. She consumed them faster than most people and could never afford to purchase enough to keep her appetite sated. So, rather than risk her next novel fix, she sucked it up, packed her things, and left her job without telling her ex-boss where to shove it.

She shifted the box to get better access to the deep fathoms of her purse, sending her emergency, backup deodorant spilling onto the ground. It rolled under the car. Her breath huffed out.

"Seriously? Whatever possessed me to buy cylindrical pit-stick?"

Latching onto her keys at last, she slid the key into the lock, opened the door, and tossed the box over the driver's seat and onto the floor on the opposite side of her metallic green, battered, vintage 1968 Dodge Charger. Her tattered canvas purse followed. She was tempted to leave the deodorant behind, but she was out of a job and had to watch her pennies until she found a new one. With the current economic recession, suitable employment, any employment, would be a limited commodity. Sure, there was employment insurance, but she was loath to take money from the government; she'd rather be working. Besides, it took weeks for Canadian government employment insurance to kick in. Maybe one of the local bookshops was hiring.

Ruing the certain damage to her silk stockings, she knelt beside the open door of her aged sedan to peer under the car. There it was, just out of reach. Maybe if she hunkered down a bit, she'd reach it. Straining, she reached forward, her fingertips just touching the offending toiletry, sending it rolling farther away.

"Fudge." Flattening herself, she inched under the car, stretched out as long as she could, and tried again. She could live without stockings. Deodorant, not so much.

Something ping-thunked against the car. She jerked her head up, crashing it painfully into the body of the car. Her glasses slipped down her nose and she jammed them back in place with an absent-minded gesture.

"Double-fudge." Agony ripped through her right temple.

She jerked to her feet, massaging the sore spot, and scanning the area. A gaggle of middle-schoolers playing in the park across the street completely ignored her. Maybe they'd been throwing rocks. She gave them a closer look. She knew them all, and there wasn't a troublemaker in the group. Couldn't have been them. Somebody must have thrown something and ducked out of sight.

A sharp crack sounded, and the back, side window exploded. Shards of glass flew everywhere. Her face stung. Something embedded itself in her arm. Sharp booming concussions rang out. Gunshots? Here, in town? She recognized the sound from her one visit to the gun range. Holy crap, they were way louder without hearing protection. Heart pounding, she dropped back to her knees, wincing at the pain ringing in her ears. Television had not prepared her for the terrifying reality of random gunfire.

Terrorized screaming of children blasted from the park. Oh my God! What if one of them got shot? Another volley of gunfire sent the kids scattering in all directions. She screamed at them to get inside, dove into her car, jammed the key at the ignition twice before realizing she was trying to start the car with her house key. She sucked in a calming breath, shoved the proper key in, cranked the car over, jammed it in reverse, and squealed out of the parking lot. She didn't know who was shooting or what they were aiming at, but she wasn't hanging around to find out.

Her tires squealed around the first corner. She took the second left, and the car tipped alarmingly. Way too fast! She didn't dare slow down. Her heart pounded triple-time before it froze and spots danced before her eyes.

Quadruple fudge! She wouldn't faint. No way! No how!

She sucked in three deep breaths. Surely, she was safe now.

She glanced in the rear-view mirror. A dark SUV careened toward her and slammed into her back end, jolting her forward. Her head slammed into the steering wheel. Pain reverberated down her neck into her shoulders. *Crap on a cracker.* Thank God her ancient car didn't have airbags. She rubbed the fresh lump rising on her forehead. It seemed enormous but not enough to keep her from fleeing. Some minor, still functioning part of her mind told her that whoever was behind her car meant business. She'd never get away in town. Too many obstacles and pedestrians.

Maybe she could escape on the highway. Forcing her foot down on the accelerator, she propelled the car faster and hightailed it out of town. Heart pounding, she fishtailed onto the highway and headed north.

Her rear window exploded into a million pieces, showering the back of her head with glass. What the heck? Weren't front and rear windows harder to break than sides? She'd have to look it up if she ever got out of this mess.

She didn't know who was chasing her, but too many unusual events seemed strangely interconnected. Her bank accounts had been drained, she'd lost her job, and now some idiot was trying to kill her. She'd annoyed someone, somehow. What could a librarian have done to piss someone off enough that they'd shoot at her and try to run her off the highway?

Another bullet slammed into the back of her car. She swerved left and right, hoping the serpentine motion would help her avoid getting shot. Thankfully there was blessedly little traffic. She veered right to avoid an oncoming car. Movies had this all wrong. It was terrifying, not exhilarating! She glanced at her fuel gauge. Shit! Barely enough gas to get anywhere. She hadn't been able to fuel up since someone had emptied her bank accounts last week. The low gas warning light had come on two days ago. She'd only driven to work to pick up the contents of her office after being terminated over the phone.

Where to go, where to go? A hundred locations jumped through her mind, none of them with suitable hiding places. That's what happened when you lived in a farming town—lots of fields, not enough trees.

Quarry Road seemed her best bet. If she could get far enough ahead of them, she might be able to lose them in the forested, rocky area. She jammed the accelerator down and pushed the pedal to its limit. The engine squealed. If she didn't let up soon, she'd blow a belt or push a rod through the side of the engine.

"Screw it." She swerved again. "A functioning car won't be of any value if someone shatters my skull with a bullet. Come on, Josie. You can make it." She encouraged herself. "Brake going into the curve, accelerate out." For the first time ever, she was glad she'd taken race car driving lessons with her adrenaline junkie, Nascar-obsessed ex.

Quarry Road was just around the next corner. If she could get far enough ahead, she might lose them in the turns. She rounded the curve, the engine and tires protesting with every motion. She slammed on the brakes at the last second and fishtailed onto Quarry Road. She punched it again and disappeared out of sight around another corner.

The sedan sputtered and stalled. She coasted to a stop behind a big pile of boulders, grabbed her purse, and looped it diagonally over her shoulder and across her body. She hopped out of the car and scrambled through the barbed wire fence. The barbs grabbed at her hair, snagging it. She jerked forward, certain she was leaving chunks of her scalp behind, and bolted into the forest.

Branches reached out and tore at her clothing, shredding her silk stockings, snagging her mohair sweater, and destroying her once-pristine linen skirt and blouse. A branch snapped against her face, just below her eye. Blood coursed down her cheek.

She pushed on, running and dodging until her lungs gave out.

Hunkering down behind an impenetrable patch of willows, she gasped and tried to still her breathing, ears perked for any sound. For a moment, there was nothing, save the erratic pounding of her heart and her frantic breathing. Gradually, she regained her calm and equilibrium. The silence was deafening.

A bird called, then another. Slowly, nature came back to life, resuming its natural rhythm now that the human intruding the area had stilled.

She flopped onto her bottom, breathing deeply, working on a plan.

"What the hell is going on?" she whispered.

Tires crunched on gravel. A car door slammed, then another. In the distance, she heard two, no three, male voices cursing.

"Shit." They'd found her car already.

Rising slowly, she inched her way farther into the forest, headed away from them, moving carefully, cautious not to make any sound that might alert them. The voices faded slowly into the distance. Still, she crept forward, increasing the distance between herself and her pursuers.

Why were they chasing her? Crap like this only happened in the movies. This wasn't a small-town occurrence. Nobody in a two-bit farm town like Manacle Beach was hunted down like this. She didn't even know what she'd done. Refusing to give in to the fatigue dragging at her, she battled slowly forward, wracking her brain for answers.

"There!"

The exclamation came from behind her.

A shot rang out. Bark exploded from the tree beside her. She flattened herself to the ground, and crawled further away.

She doubled her efforts. Survival instinct kicked in, and she fled as fast as her adrenaline-fueled legs could carry her. She stumbled, fell, and dragged herself to her feet, limping along in her high heels as best she could, while shots peppered the trees around her. Lucky for her, her enemies were terrible shots. Didn't they know that only practice and countless hours spent at the range resulted in precision shooting skills? Didn't people research anything?

Pushing forward, she stumbled out of the trees into a boulder-strewn canyon. The wall wasn't high, probably only thirty feet, but it surrounded her on three sides. She couldn't go back the way she'd come, the only way out of her predicament was—up!

"Son of a…"

Hunkering down behind a boulder, she scanned the cliff for the easiest possible route up. Too bad her ex hadn't ever forced her to take rock climbing. She could use those skills right now. It would have to be fast and easy, or she'd never make it. And if she didn't start now, she'd be caught for sure. And these stupid heels weren't going to help. What a moronic idea wearing them to clean out her desk. *Wear your best clothes, dress like you are unfazed, show them they can't get you down, and you'll win the battle.* Fudge! Considering her situation, her morning thoughts were a total load of claptrap.

Making a break for it, she dodged around rocks and sprinted forward. She grabbed her first handhold and reached for the second. Bullets ricocheted off the cliff beside her.

Too close. Her chest squeezed, and her throat closed, making her lightheaded. Forcing herself to breath deeply, she climbed higher.

She wedged one now-battered high-heeled, summer sandal into a crack and reached up with her left hand. She managed to scale another six or seven feet before three more bullets hit the wall. Something slammed into the outside of her thigh. The pain was crippling. Her leg hung useless. Biting back a cry, she dashed tears from her eyes. Getting shot hurt like hell. *Okay, think. Think, Josie.*

You've read about climbing. Right! Three points in contact with the wall all the time. Make that two since my leg is half numb. She steadied her other leg and reached up with her right hand. Over and over. She repositioned her foot and hands. Time sped by as she crawled upward. She could practically feel whoever was chasing her breathing down the back of her neck.

CHAPTER 2

Gabriel Gatlin paused mid-step. Was that gunfire?

"Damn kids." He jogged up the porch steps and grabbed his rifle from inside the door. Sprinting back toward the horse he'd tied to the picket fence surrounding his yard, he untied and mounted the brown and white stallion in one smooth motion and took off toward the quarry at a gallop.

You'd think that living ten miles from town would be enough to deter most kids. But nope. The quarry was just too perfect a place for target practice, even if it was private property. His property. He wasn't going to allow any damned kids to scare his cattle half to death.

One hand holding his tan Stetson in place, he rode, hell-bent-for-leather until he reached the edge of the canyon. He dismounted as he reined in and tossed the reins to the ground, knowing Buck-shot would stand fast and not take off. Hundreds of hours had gone into the breaking and training of his hunting horse. Nothing spooked Buckshot.

He grabbed his rifle from the scabbard on the saddle, cocked it, and strode to the canyon edge, prepared to fire off a warning shot to get the trespassers' attention.

More shots rang out. He scanned the canyon. He couldn't see anyone. Male voices called out. Two shots ricocheted off boulders at the base of the wall. He glanced down.

"What the hell?"

A red-haired woman in a tattered skirt and—were those heels? —hung precariously off the wall below him. Josie Lyons. The pretty librarian from town. What the hell was she doing? They were shooting at her!

Instinctively, he fired a single shot, well over their heads, letting them know she was no longer helpless. He raced back to his horse for a rope. Knotting it around himself, he tossed the other end over the cliff to dangle just above Josie.

"Grab the rope. I'll pull you up."

She stared up at him, her gaze flitting between him and the rope and then to the trees behind her. Even from this height, the panic and uncertainty shone in her eyes. She didn't know if she could trust him.

"Grab it, before they hit you."

"They already did," she groaned and reached for the rope. She snagged the loop on the end of the rope and wrapped it around her wrist.

Gabe tugged gently and peered over the edge. She dangled precariously from one hand and one foot. "I'll walk backward and pull you up. Help as much as you can." A bullet pinged off a rock to his left. "Hurry. We don't have much time."

His heart thundered in his ears as he inched backward. The rope pulled tight around his waist, grinding the fabric of his shirt cruelly into his skin. Below him, the woman grunted and moaned. His muscles bunched and cramped, complaining at the strain. He was fit, but he hadn't seen action like this since the army. Lord, help him. Memories thrashed at him, threatening to wipe away the present and drag him into the past. He didn't have PTSD, but, on rare occasions, his time in the service haunted him.

"Pull." Her hysteric words jerked him to the present, and he stepped back again. Her fingers clung to the edge, the wrist wrapped in the rope swollen and red from lack of circulation.

Pivoting in circles, he moved toward her, tightening up the rope as he went. At the edge, he trapped the rope under his foot and then his knee as he dropped to the ground.

"I'm going to pull you over the top. This is going to hurt." He snatched her wrist and, with one explosive movement, heaved her over the edge and dropped to the ground, taking her with him.

A bullet whistled past his ear.

"Damn. We have to move." He squeezed the words out between breaths. "This way." Crawling and yanking on her unbound arm, he guided her away from the ledge to solid ground, reducing the visibility of those below them. He clicked his tongue three times, and Buckshot trotted over to them, safely out of bullet range.

Rolling onto his side, facing her, he reached for her wrists.

She slammed one fist into his chin and clobbered him on the side of the head with the other. His teeth slammed together, and his ears rang; she packed one heck of a wallop. She'd damned near knocked him out! What the hell?

"Hold, up. I'm trying to help. I'm not with them." He rolled away from her, jumped to his feet, and backed away.

"Who the hell are you?" She struggled to stand, without taking her eyes off him. She straightened her glasses and glared.

"I'm Gabe. Gabe Gatlin. I live here." He waved in the direction of his house. "What's going on? Why are they shooting at you?"

Her breath shuddered out. "I don't know. I was in town, loading my car and—" She choked back a sob. "Shit." She sucked in a breath, closed her eyes and then blinked. "I'm okay." Another breath. "I don't have a freaking clue what's going on."

She stared at him, her brown eyes sparkling with anger and shadowed by fear. Her hand fumbled to release the rope from around her wrist.

"Josie, can I get the rope off for you?" He reached cautiously toward her. She tentatively offered her arm, and he worked the rope from around her wrist without fully freeing her hand. As he worked, he warned her, "This is going to hurt worse than anything you've ever felt. I'll release it and rub the circulation back."

She nodded.

He slipped the last loops off and briskly rubbed her hand, massaging gently, helping with the blood flow. Her wrist was chaffed and scraped. An almost complete circle of skin was gone, leaving a raw open wound. It needed cleaning and bandaging.

"Son of a…" She groaned and grabbed her wrist.

"Come on. You need to step back from sight. Hang tight." He waited until she stepped away, and rifle in hand, he crawled toward the precipice. He peeked over the edge. A shot rang out, and rock shards exploded beside him. He jerked back.

"Shit. They're not giving up." Peeking out from between two large stones, he sighted his rifle and fired a warning shot. Anticipating the bevy of return fire, he ducked. When it ebbed, he sighted again. Recalling his sniper training, he paused his breathing, aimed, and fired. One man went down. He didn't have to look to know he'd hit the target dead center in the heart. A brief flash of regret for taking a life punched him in the chest. No time for remorse in a life or death situation.

He peered over the edge and caught a flash of a red ball cap in the trees. He fired beside it, his round taking a bite out of the tree. "Get off my property before I take the rest of you out," he hollered over the edge, his voice dark and dangerous. They scrambled to comply.

~

*J*osie squatted well back from Gabe. Her leg ached abominably, but she could use it, and it wasn't bleeding much. Gunfire exploded again. This time closer. Her head jerked up to stare at him. Holy hell! He was shooting back! She had to get out of here. She skittered backward.

"Stay still," Gabe hissed. "They're leaving."

Car doors slammed. Silence. Cussing.

"What's going on?" she whispered.

Gabe chuckled. "Their car won't start. They're taking off on foot." He rolled over, leaped to his feet, and picked up his rifle. He removed the magazine and emptied the chamber as he strode toward her.

Her breath exploded in a rush of relief. Thank heavens. She was safe. He'd recued her. She'd have been dead for sure if he hadn't hauled her up. "Um, thanks for…" She waved vaguely, unable to formulate her gratitude. "Thanks for saving me."

"You're welcome. My pleasure. Come on, let's get to the house and call the police."

"Can I trust you?" Panic raced through her, relief at her rescue short-lived. She was safe, for the moment, but in tarnation was he riding around with a gun and a rope?

"I'm Gabriel Gatlin. Call me Gabe." He offered his hand. "I know you don't want to trust me, but I can't see any other option at the moment." His voice was soft and conciliatory, his grey-blue eyes serious. "Come with me. We'll ride Buckshot back to the house."

She rummaged in her purse. "I've got mace."

"Sweetheart, mace is illegal in Canada. The best you could have is bear spray. But I get the point. I promise, no shenanigans. Dig out your phone and pre-dial the police if you want to, but we have to get out of here."

Her shoulders slumped. Dang. So much for that lie. She didn't even have bear spray, but it was something to consider for the future. Not that it would do any good against bullets. She sighed again and looked at Gabe, who stood ten feet in front of her.

Double dang. He was good looking. His battered, tan Stetson had somehow remained on his head in their skirmish. He wore a plaid, button-down western shirt and oh so tight jeans. Not her type at all, but was he ever yummy. She shouldn't be attracted to him. She wasn't attracted to him. She snorted at herself. She couldn't even form that thought without laughing. She'd seen him around town. He had the most kissable lips she'd seen in ages. Once or twice, she'd even debated introducing herself. He was exactly her type. Strong and handsome. He hung around with some of the local RCMP officers, so he had to be a decent guy. Right?

Okay, so he was cute with that collar-length dark-brown hair and those slate eyes. She didn't know him and was wary after the morning's events, but he had a point. She had precious few options to choose from. So, she'd go with the lesser of two evils.

"Okay then. Let's go." She shuffled backward on her butt and stumbled to her feet. Her leg stung like crazy, but it held her weight. If a bullet had hit her, the wound must be a nick and not a full hit. "Which way?"

He rose, coiled the rope and placed it and the rifle onto his saddle. "It'll be faster if we ride Buckshot."

"No! Heck no. Double heck no, and no way." Get on a horse? Never. Especially not in a skirt. And right behind him, riding tandem snuggled up to his backside? Was his backside as fine as his front? Shoot. Adrenaline let down was making her crazy. "I'll walk. Just point me in the right direction."

"Hop on. We can call the police from the house and maybe get them out here before your *friends* disappear."

"So, I'll call the police on my cell." She rummaged around in her purse, extracted her phone, and looked at it. "Dead battery." She glared at the useless item.

He shrugged and handed her his cell. "Dial away if it makes you less wary of me. Come on, let's just go. Really, how much worse can your situation get?"

"The police say never let your attacker take you to a secondary location. It reduces your chances of survival significantly." She gave him her best "so-there" look.

"First, I am not your attacker. Second, I already saved your butt. And third, I'm going home. Stay or come. It's your choice." He gestured toward his enormous black horse and looked at her, waiting.

She looked at him, back at the ridge and at her feet. What to do? What to do? Could she take a chance on him? Could she afford not to? Her brain ran through scenarios faster than she thought possible. Death, dismemberment, rape, or worse. Good gravy, she watched too many police shows, and she was definitely giving up true crime novels. What if he was trying to help?

"Come on, Josie, we need to call the police before they disappear altogether.

"Fine." She huffed out a breath and looked at him. She wasn't going to enjoy this ride. "How do we do this?"

"Put your left foot in the stirrup. I'll grab your waist and boost you up. That leg's got to sting like crazy. I'll help you mount, and I'll climb up after. You jump and swing your right leg over the horse. Easy as pie."

She gave him a skeptical look but put her foot in the stirrup anyway. His hands landed lightly on her waist, and he counted. "On three. One, two, three. Lift." He helped her jump.

"Ooof." She slammed into Buckshot's side and stumbled back to the ground. "Well, that worked like crap." At this rate, walking would be faster. She'd never manage to get up on the enormous horse. She was five foot six, but Buckshot seemed to tower two feet above her. Whatever possessed this man to want to ride a horse?

"Jump harder. Put all your effort into it. Maybe lift your skirt a bit to give yourself more leg motion. The skirt is hindering your swing."

His gaze traced her legs from the tip of her toes to the hem of her skirt and lingered there. He might as well have run his fingers up her leg. Shivers danced across her skin leaving her breathless. Geez. When had a man's look ever affected her like that? Never, that's when. Was he right, though? Would lifting her skirt give her more leg motion? She sighed. Probably.

"Close your eyes."

"What?" His gaze shifted from her thighs to her face.

"Close your eyes. I'll lift my skirt and hop up."

"Are you serious? Time is of the essence here."

"So, stop stalling. Close your eyes, get ready, and we'll try again on three."

He groaned, closed his eyes, and gripped her waist.

She wiggled her snug skirt up, exposing her thighs and the bottom of her panties before reaching for the pommel. "One, two, three." She jumped higher this time, and even with his help, she barely managed to get her leg over the horse.

"Well done." He climbed in front of her with grace born of endless practice. "We'll gallop to the house. It'll be a rough ride. Ready?"

"Yes." She slid closer to him, his back was warm against her chest, and slung her arms around his waist.

His hips and backside strained her legs wider apart. She wanted to back away, but fear held her in place. She'd never been on a horse before, and she was afraid to relax, or open her eyes.

"Relax. It'll only take a few minutes. By the way, you have nice legs." A chuckle rumbled through his chest, up her arms and into her body. It settled somewhere low in her belly.

"You looked." She squeaked the words out. Flustered by his comment, she barely noticed when he kicked the horse into motion. The abrupt movement stalled her objections to his peeking. What had made her think she could trust this man? Sure, he'd hauled her butt out of the line of fire and was as sexy as all-get-out. But she didn't know him from a hill of beans. He could be a serial killer for all she knew, or part of the group who seemed determined to terminate her existence.

She reined in her wayward imagination. She'd seem him having coffee several times with Devlin Duke, an RCMP officer, so he couldn't be all bad. Maybe he *was* one of the good guys.

She bounced up and down, the motion of the horse sending her careening this way and that. She gripped his waist tighter, pulling herself as close as she could until she was plastered against his back like a wet shirt. This was so humiliating.

"Relax, city girl. Just sit still and move with the horse. Stop fighting him. The ride will be smoother that way. Trust me. I've spent thousands of hours on a horse. I'm going to speed up now."

"I'm not a city girl. I just don't like horses." She pinched her eyes shut, praying she'd survive this venture.

The pounding of horse hooves increased in frequency. Then, before she knew it, they were slowing down. She peeked open her eyes and glanced around him. They were coming up to a massive house.

Two stories high with dormer windows in the attic. It was painted pristine white with dark green shutters and had a wraparound porch. "Wow!"

"Like it?"

"It's beautiful." It had a warm welcoming look, especially the over-sized porch swing and all the pots brimming with colorful begonias, pansies, petunias, and lobelia. Two enormous peonies flanked the front steps. A man with flowers this lovely couldn't be all bad. *Maybe he has a wife?* Someone should write a book on the gardening habits of serial killers.

He reined the horse to a stop. "Grab my hand and swing down. I won't let you fall."

She reached out with her uninjured hand. The other ached like crazy. She grasped his hand and slid safely to the ground. She wobbled, staggered, and nearly fell. Before she hit the ground on her backside, he was beside her, grasping her arms gently, holding her up. Heat rose in her face. She couldn't even ride a horse without falling.

"Relax. It's adrenaline let down. The immediate stress is gone, and your body is unwinding. I'll help you inside, and we'll call the police." His grip shifted until it was just a warm hand on one of her elbows. It was both comforting and helpful.

Before she knew it, they were inside his home. He flicked the deadbolt closed and helped her into a chair alongside an enormous oak kitchen table. He placed the gun on the counter and studied it as if he wondered if he should let it go.

Josie ignored his actions, studying the house. It was huge. The family sized table sat at least ten. The kitchen was a chef's dream—gleaming cabinets, industrial appliances. To the right were two sets of stairs; one set led to the second floor and another to the basement. To the left, through a wide, arched doorway she saw a living room with a large leather couch and a battered and abused recliner of an indeterminate color. Clearly it was his, or someone's favorite chair. His voice startled her back to the present. He was on the phone.

"Yeah, Dev? You need to get some men out to the old gravel quarry. ASAP. I found a woman trapped there and some guys, four or five maybe, shooting at her. I hauled her up the cliff and brought her back to the house. I shot one of them." He paused. "Yes, he's dead. We'll wait here for you." He listened a moment, said good-bye, and hung up.

"Dev?" She raised one brow in query.

"Devlin Duke. He's with the police." He turned his back and rummaged in the fridge. He turned back with a jug of juice and poured two glasses, setting one on the table in front of her.

"I know who he is." She gulped the juice down gratefully. "Thanks." She set the glass down, wincing at the pain in her wrist. "Is there somewhere I can wash up? I need to clean this before it gets infected."

"No. I don't have running water," he dead-panned.

She gaped at him before snapping her mouth closed.

"Got ya." He laughed. "You can wash up. Third door on the left." He nodded toward a hallway on the opposite side of the kitchen from the living room. "You clean up, and I'll get the first aid kit."

She slipped out of her shoes and glanced at them sadly. She wasn't much for heels, but these had been her favorite power-shoes. They were ruined. The left heel was crooked and scarred. They'd never be the same. Bummer. She winced at the shallow thought. She was alive, and that was good; her favorite shoes were a small price to pay for her life.

Inside the bathroom, she closed the door and leaned against it. She was shaking like a leaf. Gabe was right. Adrenaline dump. Fight or flight response. She'd studied the body's chemical reactions when she thought was wanted to be a nurse. It would pass in a while. Breathing slowly and deeply, she reached for calm. The immediate danger was over, and if Gabe knew Devlin, he couldn't be all bad, and at least Dev knew where she was, even if he didn't know who Gabe had rescued. Okay, enough delaying. She stepped up to the sink and glanced at her reflection in the mirror.

Dear God, she was a wreck. Her perfect chignon was long since gone, and her hair stuck up in every direction. The few pieces left in her once fancy updo were decorated in sticks, leaves, and dirt. Her face was dusty, her glasses filthy. She looked like the walking dead had gone five rounds with an attack bush. Muddy tracks trailed from her eyes and nose to her chin. She must have been crying, though for the life of her, she couldn't remember doing so. All she recalled was the shooting and the sheer panic overwhelming everything. She rinsed her glasses under the tap and set them on the counter to air dry.

Her blouse was destroyed. Snagged and torn, it was beyond repair. She glanced down. Her skirt was hiked up around her waist. It must have ridden even higher after she dismounted that stupid horse. She tugged it down, doing her best to restore it to some semblance of order. It was as bad, if not worse, than her shirt. Dang. Her silk stockings were in shreds.

Crap! She realized she'd exposed her entire legs, including her stockings and garters, to Gabe's view. Heat and mortification flooded her face. Fudge it all. Why had she decided to put on her power-stockings and garter today? Just because she didn't want to show her stupid ex-boss weakness. Some women had power suits. She had power lingerie. And between the rips in her shirt and her raised skirt, Gabe had seen practically all of it.

A soft knock sounded on the door. "Josie? I've brought you something to change into, and there are cloths and a hairbrush in the cabinet. Use anything you need. I'll meet you in the kitchen."

She opened the door a crack and reached out.

He pushed gently against the door. "Are you crying?"

"No," she sobbed, unable to stop the sudden onslaught of emotion and tears.

He reached past her and set the clothing on the long, granite-topped vanity and drew her into his arms. He patted her back awkwardly. "Hey, city girl, it'll be okay. You're safe now."

She collapsed into his embrace and sobbed against his chest. Shudders wracked her body. She cried until no more tears would come. "I don't know what's going on," she mumbled into his chest. "Who would want to shoot me?"

"I don't know. Dev'll get to the bottom of it. I swear it. And if he doesn't, I will."

She looked at him, the promise and optimism in his eyes

warmed her. "Okay." She could barely push the word out. She was stretched beyond her limits.

She stared up at him, finding comfort in his serious expression. His head tilted left and he leaned forward a fraction of an inch. Was he was going to kiss her? Would she let him? The full curve of his lip was infinitely kissable. A flicker of fantasy of kissing him scrolled through her mind…until he stepped back, clearing his throat.

"Get changed. The clothes are my sister's. Wash up. Shower if you want. And we'll clean that wrist and those scrapes and the wound on your leg."

"My leg?" In the aftermath of everything, she'd forgotten the pain in her leg. She looked down, twisting so she could see the back of her thigh. "Holy shoot. Did I get shot?"

Gabe waved for her to turn so he could see the wound. He dropped to one knee for a closer look. "Grazed maybe; it's barely even bleeding. It's not a real gunshot wound."

"Close enough for me." She laughed a bit hysterically.

He rose and patted her on the shoulder. "Get cleaned up, city girl."

"Josie. My name is Josie." She pushed lightly on his chest, eased him out of the bathroom, and closed the door gently.

"I know who you are, Josie. I asked Devlin." His chuckle disappeared down the hall.

He'd asked Devlin about her? Why? Was he interested in her? She flushed at the thought, washed up quickly, restored some order to her hair, brushing out the debris and confining it in a ponytail with the elastic that had somehow survived today's ordeal. Her thigh and wrist hurt like blue blazes, and she cleaned them as best she could. She slipped into the loose shorts and cami Gabe had left her. She'd put the sweatshirt on after he helped doctor her injuries. She tossed her clothing and ruined stockings into the trash. Her garter belt looked like it might be salvageable; she scrunched it into a small plastic bag she found under the cupboard.

With her hand resting on the doorknob, she paused. She could do this. She could face this stranger, this man who'd saved her life. She would not be embarrassed that he'd seen her unmentionables or that he seemed to appreciate her legs. Gabe had rescued her. There was no way in hell she was going to admit, even to herself, that she was attracted to him. Everyone knew that relationships formed in stressful times inevitably ended in a fiery crash. Nope, she wasn't going to crash and burn with this Gabe. She did, however, owe him the courtesy of politeness at least—and probably, no definitely, more than that. She'd bide her time until Devlin arrived. Then she'd graciously thank her savior and host and leave.

Mentally fortified, she returned to the kitchen.

CHAPTER 3

Josie peeked inside each room on her way back to the kitchen, curiosity overcoming manners. Two large bedrooms; one decorated in blues and the other in shades of ivory, and one very masculine office. The third bedroom sported an enormous king-sized bed with an extra thick mattress. She'd need a stool to climb onto it. It was the picture of decadence and luxury with plush burgundy bedding and piles of pillows. In addition to these rooms, there was a staircase down the hallway, past the bathroom. Gabe's house was enormous. Two staircases led to the upper floor, one at each end of the house. What a great place for kids to run and play; they'd have a blast running laps up and down the stairs.

Why did he live in such a huge house? Was he married? Where were the other occupants? Were there other occupants? The myriad of questions made her dizzy. She wasn't nosy by nature, but something about this man made her want to know everything about him. This wasn't good; she was not attracted to Gabe. She refused to allow herself to be interested in him.

She paused at the end of the hallway, leaned against the wall, and watched Gabe working at the sink. The man had a glorious backside; those Wranglers cupped his posterior in all the right ways. Yum. Long, lean, denim-encased legs ended in sexy bare feet. Where had his boots and socks gone? She could have sworn he was wearing cowboy boots earlier. His shoulder and arm muscles bunched and flexed under the snug cotton of his shirt. The man was all country and all casual and so not what she wanted in a man, but sweet heaven, he was gorgeous from behind. Huggable. He was definitely huggable.

He turned and grinned at her. "Welcome back. Enjoying the view?"

Heat flooded her face, and she turned away, staring out the window on the opposite side of the kitchen. "Um, thanks for the clothes."

"You're quite welcome. Come and sit. I'll help you clean up those injuries. And I'd like to take a few pictures of them to show Dev what they looked like before we cleaned them. If that one on your thigh is a gunshot, he needs to know."

"Should we wait for him?" She turned toward Gabe. "Maybe he should see them first."

"I work part-time as a civilian security contractor for the police. Any pictures I take will be admissible in court if it goes there."

"I've never heard of that." She raised one eyebrow and gave her best doubtful look.

"Few people have. Mostly its for concerts, visiting politicians and dignitaries, that sort of thing. Last month, I was a bodyguard for a local country music icon doing a charity gig."

"So, that's what you do, then? For a living?"

He laughed out loud. His deep chuckle tickled down her back, leaving warmth in its wake. A small dimple appeared in his left cheek when he grinned. Dang, too cute.

"Heck no. I'm a rancher. I run a thousand head on average. I just pick up the odd security gig for extra cash and entertainment. And to help out Dev."

"That's a lot of cows. Does your wife help out?" Her eyes widened in shock at her own temerity.

Gabe laughed. "Is that your not-so-subtle way of asking my marital status?"

She squirmed under his scrutiny. "I'm sorry. I apologize. It's really none of my business. Forget I said anything. Sometimes I can't control my wayward mouth." She looked at the floor. Please, just let him drop the subject.

"I'm flattered that you asked. I'm single. I bought the house from my folks when they moved to Arizona. They still spend summers here. The ranch is mine, though my three siblings have small shares. I'm not married, nor do I have a girlfriend or children. I'm not currently dating anyone, and Devlin in my best friend. I've got two cattle dogs and more barn cats than I can count. Now, quit stalling and come over here so we can see to your injuries."

The screen door squeaked and someone pounded on the door.

Gabe walked silently to the door and peered through the peephole before opening it to admit Devlin. Gabe stepped back and Devlin strode in and stood there, hands on his hips, intimidating and masculine in his sheriff's uniform.

Before either of them could speak, Dev did. "Josie? What the hell are you doing here? And what happened to you? Jesus, you look like hell."

"Hi, Dev." She groaned at his assessment of her appearance. She wasn't vain, exactly, but she did take a certain pride in her looks. "Gabe rescued me, I guess." She shrugged. "Someone started shooting at me in town, and I took off down the highway." Her voice trembled. Dang. They'd think she was a weak, emotional female.

"I heard about the shots in town. We were investigating them when Gabe called. Nobody was hurt. The kids from the playground told me they scattered when you yelled. They're all fine, thanks to you."

"Thank God." Guilt hit her hard for not even thinking about anyone else, especially the kids in the park. When her window shattered, all she could think about was getting away from whatever was going on. So many people could have been hurt. Or killed. *I could have been...* She swallowed back a lump of shame and terror.

"Come on, girl." Dev wiped his boots and waved her toward the table where Gabe had a basin of soapy water and first aid supplies waiting. "Let's get some pictures of those wounds and clean them up while you tell me what happened."

Reluctantly, she left the hallway and moved to the table. Dev took pictures of her injuries with his department issue camera, and she dropped into a chair, unable to stand any longer on her shaking knees. At his urging, she started relating the morning's events. Dev made notes while Gabe cleaned the scratches on her legs.

"Obviously, this isn't what you were wearing. Where are your clothes? I'll need them for evidence. There probably won't be anything, but we can't risk overlooking something important. It's procedure."

"In the trash in the bathroom." She waved vaguely in that direction. "Except this..." She held up the bag holding her garter belt. "This was the only thing worth salvaging. Do you need it?" Her face flushed, and she looked away.

"What is it?" Dev asked.

Gabe's touch was gentle as he wiped more dirt from her wounds. Biting pain ripped through her leg where the bulled had nicked her right thigh. "Ouch. Dang it, be careful." She glared at Gabe. "Give a girl some warning at least."

"It's probably her teal garter belt." Gave winked at her.

Heat rose in her face again. Sweet heaven, if any more blood rushed to her face, her head would explode. Why didn't the floor just open up and swallow her?

Dev choked back a laugh. "I think it's okay. Just don't wash it until the investigation's over, just in case we need it."

"Fine. It's not like there's DNA on it or anything. I don't know why you want my stuff."

"Proof of injury for one thing. You never know what small piece of evidence might come in handy at a trial. A couple years ago, a broken pair of eyeglasses was the tipping point on convicting a man who murdered his wife." He paused and rubbed his chin before crossing his arms over his chest. "I'm not sure why they're after you, but I will find out. Just point me in the direction of your clothing so I can process them."

"Okay. If you say so." She was fast reaching the point where all she wanted was to be left alone to nap. Her limbs trembled with exhaustion. As important as the endless stream of questions was, she was fed up. She braced herself for more. Dozens of questions followed, one after another with Devlin frequently requesting more information or clarification.

"Okay, I think I have enough to go on. I have a team down in the quarry. I'll let you know what we find out. Stay inside until we know what's going on. I want you here, out of the way, in case they know where you live. You," he pointed toward Gabe, "you have a big house with lots of rooms… Keep her safe and indoors and keep a firearm handy."

"I'll keep them in close reach."

"This is official police business. You'll be compensated for your assistance," Devlin stated.

"Like hell I will." He glanced at Josie. "Sorry. I don't typically swear like that, and certainly not in front of a lady. I'll watch her because she's my guest. Just go and get those bast—guys."

"I can go stay with Amelia." Her best friend would take her in without question. She was meeting Amelia for lunch, if she didn't check in with her, Amelia would pitch a fit worrying.

"I want you to stay here, out of sight. If someone is gunning for you, we can't risk you being seen in town."

She pondered his words and reluctantly agreed to stay on the ranch. "I'll stay, I'll call Amelia and let her know I'm okay."

"Tell her to keep it to herself," Devlin advised. "We want to keep this as quiet as we can." He winced. "Not that keeping the gossip grapevine is possible in a small town."

Ten minutes later, Devlin was gone, and Josie sat at the table, wounds bandaged, searching for something to say beyond thank you. She'd already thanked Gabe half a dozen times, and her inability to make conversation was getting embarrassing. Now that they were alone, she was nervous and uncertain and scared to death. Not of Gabe, but of her circumstances Who would shoot at a nobody like her? Gabe paced the kitchen.

"Come into the living room, and I'll build a fire. You're shaking like a leaf in a tornado. You must be frozen. Shock does that. We'll get you warmed up, and I'll make a hot drink."

She followed him into the adjacent room, settled on the couch, and let him cover her with a thick, soft, blue and white quilt. The leather couch was plush and comfortable. It faced an enormous picture window with small casement windows on either side that would open and allow fresh air into the room. Another large window took up most of the side wall—was that north? Between the front door, the kitchen windows, and living room windows, she had an almost horizon to horizon view. Only the wall behind the couch was window free, though there was a small casement in the corner. Being able to see what was coming and having her back to the wall gave her a measure of comfort. They wouldn't be sneaking up on her here.

Gabe built a fire in the enormous fireplace nestled between the two big windows. Warmth blazed out almost instantly. He stood and brushed his hands on his jeans, drawing her attention to the muscles of his thighs. Damn, the man filled out a pair of jeans nicely.

"Tea? Coffee?"

"Oh. Coffee, please. I think I need the caffeine to calm me down."

He reared back, appearing surprised. "Caffeine to calm down?"

"Go figure." She shrugged, dislodging the quilt from around her shoulders. "It's been like that since I was a teenager. Coffee makes me calm. Just black, please."

He re-tucked the blanket around her shoulders. Half a minute later, he was back with two steaming cups of coffee. He set the mugs on the table, nestled between the couch and battered recliner, beside a pair of field glasses. He pulled a revolver from his waistband and set it on the coffee table, checked on the fire, and sat in the recliner.

"Can you sit here? With me?" She couldn't stop herself from asking. She needed him beside her, helping her scan the horizon for unwanted guests.

"Are you sure?" He rose and moved slowly toward her. "You've been through a lot. You might not want me too close."

She snaked her arm out and grabbed her coffee. Keeping the quilt tucked over her shoulders, she managed to free both arms enough to cradle the warming cup between her hands. She took a bracing sip and closed her eyes. "I feel—exposed sitting here alone. Dev vouched for you…"

"Trauma does strange things to a person. We don't react the way we want to, and we can't control our thoughts. It's okay. I understand what you're feeling." He stopped in front of the couch. "How close?"

The question struck her as strange until she realized he was trying to determine her comfort zone. "Beside me, but not too close." It was difficult to articulate precisely what she needed. She'd crawl into his lap if it didn't make her feel like a wimp. Or if she wasn't afraid she'd attack him. This man was just a stranger to her, yet he was prepared to protect her. This hero, she owed him her life. How could she thank him? She wished they'd me under different circumstances because though he was still a stranger to her, he was a comfort to look at… to have beside her.

Whoa!

Apparently, being chased by strangers, shot at, and nicked by a bullet had knocked her senseless. She couldn't even remember the last time she'd been attracted to a man, let alone caught herself thinking about kissing one.

He settled beside her, close enough to touch if she leaned in a little, but far enough away she didn't feel crowded. He'd found the perfect distance, seemingly without trying. Could he read her that well? She wasn't usually so transparent.

CHAPTER 4

*B*eing around Josie was like walking through a minefield. She needed comfort, without him scaring her to death. He had to protect her and be near her without compromising his awareness of their surroundings. Mix that with the fact that he wanted to protect her? But he was aware of her beauty, and he hadn't had a girlfriend in a long time. One look at her lit a fire inside his heart. However, his need added up to inconvenience. He was a man with manly emotions. He had to stamp out these more masculine emotions if he was going to protect her. He might not like having to hold back after being attracted to her for so long. Hell, it was a pain in his hind end. If it wasn't for his army training teaching him to ignore distractions and focus on the immediate situation, he'd be totally lost in staring at her. As it was, he could barely keep his focus on her safety.

The heat radiated from her body. The urge to get closer, to pull her into his arms, battered him. He pushed the need aside and drank his coffee, forcing his attention away from her light, enticing smell, to the yard. How could she smell that nice after a day like she'd had?

He scanned the yard from tree line to tree line. It was doubtful her attackers would know where the house was, or who'd rescued her, unless they were local, which seemed unlikely. But, in time, their search could lead them right to his front porch. He had to be prepared for that.

While she was changing, he'd moved Buckshot to the barn and placed a loaded rifle, safety on, under the couch. Similarly, there was a gun handy in the kitchen and in his bedroom. Innate optimism told him he wouldn't need them, but better safe than sorry. He picked up a cordless phone off the side table.

"Who are you calling?"

"My foreman, Jake, an old army buddy. I'm telling him what's going on and sending the rest of the hands home, or having them hole up in the bunkhouse. Jake'll keep watch. He's trained. The other guys—not so much. They're great workers and amazing with the horses and cattle, but none of them have police or military training. So, we'll keep them out of harm's way."

He made the call and handed out orders, quickly, concisely and politely, yet left no doubt he was as serious as the situation. Gabe's commander had praised his people skills on the day Gabe had handed in his resignation. His commander and those above him had wanted Gabe to move into the officer training program, hoping to have him lead troops overseas. But he'd done his time, and his heart yearned for the ranch he'd grown up on. His resignation stood, and he'd been home for three years. And unattached for every moment of that time. Not once had he been tempted by a local woman, until the day he'd seen Josie outside the grocery store, six months ago.

He hadn't asked anyone who she was. He believed in serendipity. If they were meant to meet, their paths would cross again. Sooner or later, they'd bump into each other. Like today. Only this wasn't how he'd envisioned it. His visions had entailed flirting, picnics, and plenty of kissing that led to more interesting pursuits. Those games would have to come later, if at all. There were more serious issues to attend to.

"What are game cameras? You mentioned them when you were on the phone."

"I have a dozen motion-activated cameras strategically placed around the ranch. They turn on when a large animal or person passes them. The images are recorded as long as the motion continues. While it wasn't their purpose, the cameras may warn us if anyone approaches. We had some trouble with cougars last fall. Knowing cougars are in the area allows us to get the jump on them before they take down any cattle."

"You kill them?" Her glare was adorable.

"As a last resort, yes. But as a rule, we trap them and forestry comes and relocates them. I don't believe in indiscriminate killing. I hunt and raise cattle for food, not for sport."

"That's good." She cradled her cup against her slender tummy and leaned back, closing her eyes.

Her dark auburn lashes made pretty crescents against her pale, scratched cheeks. He wished he had the power to erase the scrapes marring her lovely skin. A couple dozen freckles stood out against the pallor of her skin. He was tempted to kiss each one. She'd clock him for that, no doubt. Her appearance was deceiving. At a glance, one would guess weak or fragile, but he'd seen her inner strength and determination. His jaw still ached where she'd punched him.

She was a tough cookie. She hadn't cried or wailed about her situation, and when he arrived at the ridge, she'd been busy trying to escape rather than giving up. It said a lot for her common sense that she'd decked him first and trusted him later. He suspected that if he hadn't known Dev, she'd have hightailed it off the ranch at the first opportunity. He respected that.

What bothered him was the fact she had no explanation for being chased and someone shooting at her. It baffled him. Dev seemed to believe her, but with no explanation, the situation felt off. If she wasn't involved in criminal activity, maybe she'd overheard something, or seen something… Questions battered him, but he took the time to choose the perfect one before he spoke.

"You work in the library?" he asked. The question startled him. It wasn't the one he'd planned to ask. He was going more for history, for the reason she'd been chased.

"I do. I have a degree in Library Sciences. I'm the head librarian. Or rather, I was until my jerk boss, Ramone Garcia, canned me for no reason. Cutbacks he said. I say horse pucky. We just received an enormous grant. We've worked together for two years. Every evaluation I received has been glowing—Josie exceeds expectations. I love that job, and now I've been canned. I don't get it."

"You worked there two years?"

"Five. Garcia was hired when I turned down the administrative position. I love what I do. The books, the readers. Paperwork bores me. I like being in the stacks, helping people find the perfect book." Her love of books and reading was clear in the passion and happiness in her voice.

"Anyone have a grudge against you?"

"Do I look like the type of person people dislike?"

The annoyance stood out in her voice. He stifled a chuckle. She did have a point, but one thing he'd learned serving his country was everyone had secrets, even the innocent. There was always a part of you that nobody else ever saw.

"Dent anyone's car? Overhear any conversations, see anything you shouldn't have? Anything weird or unusual happen lately?"

"I rarely drive my car. It's only ten blocks to the library, and I'm pretty sure I'd recall hitting someone." She paused, her mouth open, poised on the brink of another denial.

"What?" He kept his tone gentle and inquisitive, avoiding sounding accusatory.

"I totally forgot until you asked about an accident. I did see one three months ago. A hit and run in the grocery store parking lot. A navy-blue SUV ran over Mikah Smith. They just ran him down.

Right over top of him and kept on going. I was the only person who came forward. I gave the police what I remembered of the license. It was awful. Blood everywhere and the sound…" She shuddered. "I'll never forget that sound. I tried to help him, but he died before the ambulance arrived." Blinking furiously, she dashed away a tear.

"What do you know about Smith?" This could be the reason she'd been targeted. If this Smith guy had a history, someone could have taken him out on purpose. Hitting a guy hard enough to kill him, in a parking lot, wasn't an easy feat. It could have been deliberate. And if she'd witnessed a hit and reported it…

"I didn't really know him. I mean, he came into the library occasionally. His preference was for travel guides and illustrated books on Russia and Chicago. He read a lot of murder mysteries, too."

"You remember what he read?"

"Manacle Beach is a small town. You know that. You live here. It's only busy in the height of summer. In winter, the place practically shuts down. Of course, I remember what he read, and everyone else. It helps with ordering new material. I might add I've never seen you in the library."

Gabe ignored her comment. "Doesn't that combination strike you as odd? Russia and Chicago?"

"Not really. People can be eclectic in what they read. Enid at the grocery story reads books on climbing Everest, scuba diving, and erotic romance." She slapped a hand over her mouth. "Oh, forget you heard that. I never should have told you, or anyone that. What you read is your business and nobody else's. That was so indiscrete."

"Enid reads erotica?" He couldn't help but laugh. Wasn't that just like the old gal? She had to be seventy and always had her nose in everyone's business. "What did Mikah do for a living? Do you know?"

She seemed to be pondering the information, clearly uncertain if she should be talking about her former client like that. "I think he was retired. He told me he was sixty-five. He moved here around the same time I did. He didn't have many friends. Nobody ever indicated disliking him, but he spent most of his time alone in the library or drinking tea at the Shackle, which is a ridiculous name for a café. It's almost as bad as calling a bar the Ball and Chain. Who names town landmarks with criminal references? I really don't know much about Mikah. It just saddened me when he was killed. Nobody deserves to die like that. Nobody."

"Did anything about him strike you as odd? Weird mannerisms, odd habits, things like that?" Something was triggering a thought process in Gabe's head. Spending time in a war zone had taught him to trust his instincts. Why would someone strike down an old man and take off? It didn't add up.

"Just that he always sat with his back to the wall in the café and read in a library corner near the emergency exit. Always that one spot, and if it was taken, he left. I suggested another quiet spot, but he claimed he was a 'creature of habit' and left. I just assumed he was OCD or something similar and didn't worry too much about it."

She hadn't looked at him while they talked. Beneath her eyelids, her eyes darted back and forth as if she was searching for memories to put the entire incident in perspective. He was impressed with her focus, though he did wonder why she trusted him.

"I can't think of anything else out of the ordinary."

Gabe wondered if she meant about Mikah or about her own life. Her lips puckered into a frown, and her eyes danced behind closed lids. The motion of her eyes slowed, and she huffed out a small sigh. Her coffee cup tilted to one side, nearly spilling the last of the liquid. He grabbed the cup and set it on the table. She didn't move.

She was asleep.

Post-adrenaline letdown. He'd been there. As a soldier, he'd been trained to deal with it, but for a civilian, it could knock you on your ass for hours or days if the fright lasted long enough. For some, they went into extended panic mode and had trouble regaining their equilibrium. It appeared Josie was coming down already. She was one tough lady.

He picked up his cell phone and texted Devlin the new information. It could be the clue he needed to find the perpetrators.

He should get up and do a perimeter check of the house, or start laundry, or put something on for supper, but it was much easier and more pleasant to watch her sleep. She was beautiful. Not in the classic sense, but more in a down-to-earth clean and healthy sense. She was fit and curvy. And her hair, damn, he'd like to tangle his fingers in those long strands. Not quite brown, not quite red, the color defied description, but it was lovely.

Forcing his attention away from Josie, he scanned the yard. Five hundred yards of grazing land lay past the lawn. Grazing land morphed into tree-covered hills. The grass under the trees was short and cow-mowed, but from this distance, a person could easily hide from anyone watching. Crossing that open stretch of field would be more difficult. If anyone approached the house, they'd have better luck under the cover of darkness. But with a rifle, anyone sitting inside would be a sitting duck. Those game cameras better catch anyone before they got too close.

He rose and closed the curtains. No sense sitting in the open. They'd be sitting ducks, or fish in a barrel.

He should rest now so he'd be alert later, but restlessness flowed through him, making him antsy. Was it the situation? A premonition? Or Josie? No matter how he sliced it, he didn't like it.

CHAPTER 5

The enticing aroma of coffee woke Josie from a deep sleep. Who was making coffee? She bolted upright, agony slamming through her abused muscles. She groaned as reality slammed back into place. Gabe's ranch. Someone had been shooting at her. Crap!

"There are a couple pain killers and a glass of water on the coffee table. I should have given them to you before you went to sleep. You should get up and move a bit, work out the kinks. It'll hurt, but it's best to move before the stiffness gets worse."

She reached out to grab the two white tablets on the table. Pain rippled across her shoulders and down her arms and back. Fudge. Moving in any fashion was going to be agony. Slowly, she rotated her shoulders and flexed her back. The pain eased but didn't disappear. "I never should have tried rock climbing."

Gabe laughed as he entered the room. He held out her coffee mug. "Coffee?"

"Thanks." She reached out cautiously to accept the cup.

"Maybe you should try rock climbing with proper gear and not in heels and a skirt?"

"That might help." She glanced around the room. The drapes had been drawn, and the lights were dim. "What time is it?"

"Nearly nine. You slept for several hours."

"And the drapes? I could've watched the sunset." She adored sunset. It was her favorite time of day. She'd sit on her apartment balcony and sip a glass of wine, watching the last rays of daylight color the sky. Sunsets with her grandfather had been the highlight of her youth, until he died when she was eighteen. They would be magnificent here with such a vast, open area to view it. All those trees and that open sky, add in some puffy clouds…splendid. She missed it.

"No sunset for you, or sunrise, either. Until Dev catches whoever did this, you're on lockdown. Blinds closed so nobody can see in. Dev found a rifle and pistol casings by your car, so we keep you hidden from everyone."

"You talked to Dev?" She hadn't heard the phone ring.

"He called while you were sleeping. I have my cell on vibrate. Didn't want to wake you."

"Oh. Did he find them?" she asked. Wouldn't that be perfect? If Dev had found her assailants and taken them into custody. He couldn't have caught them, or she wouldn't be on lockdown.

"Not yet, but he had their car impounded and yours towed into town. It's at Mercury's Garage. The police dusted it for prints and checked it over for evidence. Now, they've taped over the busted windows but won't do anything else until you call them. Not having a car will slow these guys down, at least until they get another one. Dev's guys are patrolling the highway between here and town, watching for strangers on foot."

At a loss for a response, she kept silent and sipped her coffee, searching for something to say. Nothing sprang to mind. She struggled to her feet and headed toward the bathroom. Her brain never functioned when she had a full bladder. She wandered down the hall. Even the soles of her feet hurt.

She closed the bathroom door behind her and stared at her reflection in the mirror. There was a mirror behind her, on the back of the door. Strange she hadn't noticed it before, but then she wasn't at her finest on her first trip to the room. She looked like something the cat dragged in. Her hair was askew. Her face and arms a mass of bruises and scrapes. Her legs were no better. She lifted her shirt. Her ribs were bruised, and a ten-inch scrape marred her abdomen. It glowed red in the bright bathroom lights. She'd missed it earlier and would have to clean it now.

She used the bathroom and picked up a clean cloth from the counter. Gabe must have replaced the towels and tidied up after she'd been in here. The room was spotless and the towels fresh. He'd been busy while she was sleeping.

She closed the toilet lid and settled on the seat. Her mind whirled around, conflicting thoughts hammering away at her and bumping into each other. One cancelled the other and created a dozen more questions. Why was this happening to her? What would have happened if Gabe hadn't arrived? She sucked in a frightened breath. Dear Lord, she could have died! Panic surged anew, and she battled it back with sheer will. She was safe now. Gabe was here, and he'd protect her.

Why did she feel so safe with him? She'd never have fallen asleep in a strange man's house before today, so she must trust him. Why? She hardly knew him. Sure, Dev knew him, but she'd trusted him before that. She'd started trusting him right after she'd socked him in the jaw and he'd remained calm. Good gravy! She'd punched him. More than once. Heat rose in her face. She'd have to apologize for that.

A soft knock sounded on the door. "You okay in there?"

"I'm good." Fudge. He was even keeping watch over her in the bathroom. "I'll be right out." As soon as she tamped down the embarrassment over hitting him.

"Okay. I'll put supper on the table. I hope you like chicken stew."

"Two minutes." It wasn't two minutes. It was closer to ten before she regained control of herself and entered the kitchen. The spicy aroma of stew and the yeast smell of freshly baked bread hit her instantly.

"It smells delicious." She breathed deeply to capture more of the enticing smell. "You made bread?"

He laughed. "No. I heated up some frozen rolls. My sister makes the dough and freezes it in pre-formed balls. I just thaw and bake. No effort on my part. I can cook, but baking is out of the question."

She laughed. "I can bake, but cooking is out of the question. I could live on macaroni and fresh fruit. But right now, I could eat a horse."

"Hey, leave my horse alone. Try the stew instead." He waved her toward the table.

They sat, and he bowed his head and gave a quick prayer, thanking God for their meal and for the blessing of Josie surviving her ordeal. She was surprised, but pleased. She believed in God. She just didn't go to church. She was more spiritual than religious. Believers seemed rare these days. How strange she'd stumbled upon one under such trying circumstances.

"Amen," she repeated his closing and picked up her spoon. "It looks delightful."

They ate in silence for a few minutes. A plate filled with bite-sized morsels of tender chicken and perfectly cooked vegetables; the stew was delicious. Carrots, celery, turnips and peas in a thick gravy-like broth were a perfect combination. She couldn't resist dipping her fresh buttered roll into the heavenly sauce. The morning's activities had made her ravenous. Fear made her hungry; who knew?

She glanced at him and smiled. "You've got to love a man who can cook."

"It's a bit early for love." He winked. "But I do like you. In a strange way, I'm glad you stumbled onto my ranch."

She sputtered and choked on a bite of chicken. She glared at him when the coughing sputtered to a stop. "Not funny."

"Yes, it was." He chucked. "If not the joke, then your expression of it was."

"Are you always this *funny*?"

"Actually, no. You make me want to smile and laugh."

"This is hardly the time for joking." His attitude irritated her as much as it thrilled her. When was the last time she'd been attracted to a man? Four, five years ago? Probably before she came to Manacle Beach. Sure, she'd dated once or twice, but this was a small town, a micro-town, really, and the options were limited.

"Actually, it's the perfect time to lighten the mood. You seem uptight. Some tension is good, but if we get too riled up, we release adrenaline, and we might need it later, so we joke and laugh and try not to be too tense. So, I cracked a funny. Though, in all honesty, it isn't a joke. I noticed you the first time I saw you."

She wrinkled her nose and squinted at him. "And how long ago was that?"

"A while." He flushed. "Okay, six months."

"Wow." Sarcasm dripped from the single syllable. "All that time and you never once approached me? The attraction must be *enormous*." She was irked and unusually combative. It wasn't like her to fret over things like men or dating. The circumstances were making her prickly.

"It wasn't like that. It was—hang on, I need to get this." He extracted his cell phone out of his pocket and growled a greeting into it.

His transformation was complete and instantaneous. From flirting cowboy to alert soldier. Add those to her rescuer and chef and he had way too many sides to keep track of. Who was the real Gabriel Gatlin?

"Yup. No. Okay." He spoke to the person on the other end with a series of one-word answers and disconnected.

"Dev's putting two men on the house for the night. We're to stay inside until morning and not leave until he gives us permission. He won't say why, but he thinks they'll be back. If not tonight, as soon as they realize where you are. Someone was in the library, asking questions and looking at property registrations. Your co-worker Miranda called the police."

Her spoon clattered to the table, her hands shaking. "Shoot. I was hoping Dev would catch them." Manacle Beach, a small lakeside, farming community, had a police force that covered a wide rural territory. As such, it had a large contingent of officers. Even so, she couldn't imagine Dev would position two of his men on Gabe's ranch unless he perceived the threat to her was immediate and serious.

Her gut clenched and roiled. The once-delicious stew sat like lead in her stomach, threatening to make a reappearance at any moment. Why was this happening to her? She placed her spoon in her bowl and rose. The spoon rattled against the lovely blue and white bowl. Carefully, she rinsed them and set them in the sink.

Gripping the edge of the sink with both hands, she struggled for calm. "I don't think I can do this. Maybe you should take me to town. They can lock me in the police station for the night."

The heat of his body behind her warmed her. He was close but not touching her. He'd gotten there without making a sound. Gently, he rested his hands on her shoulders. "Relax, Josie. You can do this. You escaped them once. Hell, you ran through the bushes and climbed a cliff in a skirt and heels. You're safe with me. I'm watching you inside. Two of Dev's men and Jake are patrolling outside. You're as safe here as anywhere else." He massaged her shoulders and upper back.

"I don't get it. I didn't do anything. Why are they after me? Why is Dev taking this so seriously? Maybe it was just a random shooting?" She hated the way her voice quivered, giving away her fear. It was bad enough she couldn't control her mouth. She didn't need her body betraying her, too.

"If it were random, they would have let you run and not chased you. The typical civilian would report the event and move past it, thinking they were in the wrong place at the wrong time. But they chased you. That indicates you are a target for some reason. You'll be fine here with me. The house is locked down."

"But they've got guns. Rifles! They're trying to kill me."

He gave her a little shake. "Breathe, Josie. I've got this. You'll be fine with me. You've got two choices. One, be strong and alert, or two, give in and let the panic take over and make yourself an easier target."

The harsh words hit her like physical blows.

He was right. She wasn't going to let them win. She wouldn't give them that. She'd be calm and rational, even if it killed her. She'd read enough murder mysteries to know panic never helped. And heaven knew she'd seen enough horror movies to realize the chick who went outside always got killed. She would *not* be that girl.

She took three deep breaths, grasped his hands, and removed them from her shoulders before turning around. "I'm good." She gave him her best attempt at a smile. It was wobbly and uncertain, but that was all she could manage.

"That's my girl." He gave her a quick peck on the cheek and stepped back. "We've got this. Now, let's clean up these dishes and find something funny to watch on TV. I don't have cable, but I do have Netflix. There has to be something to watch."

She touched the spot his lips had grazed. He'd kissed her. And he barely knew her. Did it mean something, or was he just being manly and reassuring? Chivalrous? She'd be danged if she knew one way or the other. What she was certain of was she liked the way her cheek tingled in the wake of his caress.

They worked in unison, side by side, and had the kitchen cleaned in no time. The mundane chore was comforting and relaxing. Occasionally, they brushed shoulders or bumped into each other. Each touch sent a thrill through her. His nearness was electrifying. It was so inappropriate and titillating she almost laughed at herself. Look at her, attracted to a stranger and having random fantasies of kissing him or leading him to the decadent king-sized bed she'd seen in the master bedroom earlier. Oh yeah, she was in trouble. Too many kinds of trouble.

CHAPTER 6

Television was a bust. She couldn't concentrate on anything, and they'd tried a dozen shows, despite the peace and safety in the dim room. Only a glowing fire in the fireplace and half a dozen candles provided light. Despite his explanation that less light kept them from being easily spotted from outside, the atmosphere was entirely too romantic. She glanced at Gabe again and again, attracted to his smile, his dimple or his sparkling eyes. She liked the way his dark brown hair grazed the collar of his T-shirt. Sometime during the day, his western shirt had disappeared, leaving him in a muscle-hugging white T-shirt. The look suited him. He was masculine, sexy, and ridiculously appealing.

Their gazes met, and he winked.

Shivers raced down her spine. His smile was amazing and alarming. She was having trouble fighting her sudden, inexplicable attraction to him. It had to be the stress. People had sexual reactions to stress, didn't they?

Whoa, Nellie! Sexual attraction? She didn't want to think of him in those terms. No way, no how. She sighed. Yeah, she was. She had been all day. He was the most attractive man she'd seen since coming to town five years ago. He'd been here three years. How had she gone that long without meeting him in a town as small as Manacle Beach? Under normal circumstances, he'd be totally drool-worthy and completely dateable. She felt safe with him. Well, she felt safe from harm, but her body and her heart were already falling for him. Could you fall for a guy in hours? Didn't tense circumstances cause atypical attractions? Was that what she was feeling? Lord help her, she was in a pickle here. She had to get away from him before she gave in to the urge to caress his forearm and see if it was as strong as it looked.

She faked a yawn. "I'm bushed. I think I'll go to bed. Which bed do I use?" She scooted off the couch and stood, looking at him.

"Come on. I'll show you." He rose and grasped her hand.

His hand was warm, strong, and calloused. It dwarfed her much-smaller one, making her feel delicate and petite when she was nothing of the sort. At five foot six, she was no tiny little thing. He squeezed her hand lightly. It felt like heaven and like he was leading her toward certain doom.

"You can sleep in my room. The sheets are clean." He guided her into the room with the plush, luxurious bed. The four-poster bed dwarfed the room. Towering spires and an ornately carved headboard and footboard spoke of old-world elegance and charm.

"No, I can't take your bed. One of the other rooms will be fine." She tried backing away, but he kept a firm grip on her.

"I won't be sleeping. This room is best. It's central. It's close to the exits, and there's a back door leading out of the far bedroom. Plus, this one has a light right outside the window. Perfect for safety. You'll sleep here."

"I don't want to put you out of your bed." She disliked his logic and his no-nonsense tone. But his reasoning made sense.

"I'm not sleeping," he repeated.

Oh golly. She was mortified. She'd exploded into his life and completely turned it higgity-piggity. He'd saved her, clothed her, and fed her, and now she was kicking him out of his bed and making him stay up all night. Would this nightmare ever end? She sighed.

"Fine." She might as well acquiesce; she had a feeling her objections would fall on deaf ears. She'd only known him for a few hours, and already she had the impression once his mind was made up, there was no shifting his position. She liked a person who took a stand and stuck to their guns. That wasn't good. Just one more reason to be attracted to him, as if there weren't enough already.

He released her hand and opened a dresser drawer. He held out a masculine, light blue T-shirt with a sports logo on it. "Here. My sister didn't leave any night clothes. You can sleep in this. There's a new toothbrush in the medicine cabinet." He nodded toward the open door to the ensuite bath she hadn't noticed.

Her mouth dropped open, and she snapped it shut, reaching out to accept the shirt. "Um. Thanks. Are you sure?" She floundered. She didn't even know what she intended to ask. If it was okay to borrow his shirt? Sleep in his bed? Use the toothbrush? Or something else entirely? The man had her off kilter with his thoughtfulness and assistance.

He nodded. "Open the door after you get changed, please. I want to be able to hear you if you need anything. Don't hesitate to call."

Minutes later, she was snuggled into his bed, hair combed and teeth brushed. She left the door open a crack as he'd requested. She'd been tempted to defy him and had struggled with the urge to close and lock the door. Only fear for her safety had changed her mind. She was more afraid of the strangers outside than the one inside. Better the devil you know—sort of. She wiggled under the covers, fluffed the pillow, and closed her eyes. And waited for sleep to come.

She was exhausted. Her body ached, and every motion was agony; every scratch felt like a knife wound and every bruise like a hammer strike. It was an effort to even think. But that didn't stop her mind from chattering away at her. She tossed and turned, fluffed the pillow again, and attempted to blank her mind. Imaginary bullets ricocheted around her. Trees scraped at her body and face. She bolted upright. Nope. This wasn't going to work. She was too keyed up to sleep. She shouldn't have had that coffee. She'd had three with supper. A cup or two was calming, but she'd exceeded that limit and careened straight into wired and high strung. She needed a drink.

She crawled off the enormous bed, slipped back into the shorts he'd loaned her earlier and padded, barefoot, into the living room. "Have you got any wine?"

"Can't sleep? I wondered if that last cup of coffee was a good idea." He stepped back from where he was peeking through the curtains into the yard, closing them tightly.

"I think all three cups were a mistake. I never drink coffee after noon. I'm more an herbal tea in the evening girl. So, do you have any?"

"Herbal tea? No. I'm a coffee man."

"Wine?" She gave him a quizzical look. "Preferably red."

"Mom might have left some here, but it's unlikely." He disappeared downstairs and returned a moment later, triumphantly brandishing a bottle. "I don't know what it is. It's called Raven, and it's wine." He shrugged and started rummaging through the drawers. "I know there's a corkscrew here somewhere. I stabbed my finger on it last week."

He opened the bottle and poured a large portion of the deep red liquid into a cut crystal wineglass.

"You don't drink wine, but you have glasses?"

"Mom's. She left pretty much everything when they moved. We still do Easter and Christmas here every year, so she left all the fancy dishes. Those glasses are her favorites. Do you need to let that breathe or something?"

She swallowed several large gulps. "Probably, but not tonight.

My need for alcohol outweighs proper wine etiquette." She laughed woodenly, as if she'd made a joke. "Join me?"

"I'd love to, with a beer. But I've got to stay alert. One glass is all you get. I can't have you liquored up and useless." His grin let her know he was teasing. "Come sit in the living room. Drink your wine and then back to bed with you."

She followed him and settled onto the couch, under the blanket in what she was already coming to think of as her spot. Forcing herself to sip slowly, she enjoyed the wine. She was tempted to down the glass in a single go and follow it with the rest of the bottle. It would knock her on her ass for what was left of the night and half of tomorrow, which felt like the perfect solution to her tension and inability to sleep. Crazy thoughts for a girl who rarely drank. She was losing her mind.

Gabe settled beside her, just close enough to touch but far enough away that he wasn't crowding her. Her errant body wished he'd come closer so she could snuggle up to his warmth and strength. She needed comfort right now, and Gabe was the perfect man to provide it. She pretended to be lost in watching the fire but kept stealing glances at him. She could tell he noticed but was gentleman enough not to mention it.

Gabe. Gabriel. An angelic name for a man who looked like he'd fallen straight from heaven. Gabriel Gatlin. Funny, Gatlin somehow made her think of the powerful Civil War invention, the Gatling Gun—again, appropriate. Dangerous but protective. An angelic man with strength, solidity and a hint of menace. She snorted at her own fanciful ideas. She was more out of sorts than she'd realized.

"Come on, girl. Finish that last mouthful, and let's get you to bed. You're asleep on your feet." He made a drink-up gesture.

"Can you sit with me?" She waited until they were at the bedroom door before she asked. Being alone would drive her crazy. Fear and loneliness had kept her awake earlier. Maybe if he sat on the bed beside her, she'd be able to sleep.

"There's no chair." His gaze darted around the room, avoiding hers.

"You can sit on the bed. Please."

~

It was the quiver in her voice that broke him. She'd been tough all day, fighting and strong. Now, in the dark of late evening, that small tremor cut deeply. He swallowed a sigh. He shouldn't be in here. He should be patrolling the house, checking windows and doors, and watching the yard for unusual activity. Sitting in the dark with her was dangerous on too many sides. He'd be derelict in his duty if he stayed.

"Climb into bed and cover up. I'll sit down here by the footboard."

She climbed into the bed and covered up. After a moment of serious wiggling, she flung the shorts she'd been wearing from under the covers. They landed against the far wall. She grinned. Her expression was playful, grateful, and seductive all at once. He was certain the last part was unintentional; she was a natural seductress without even trying. Seeing her snuggled under his covers, her dark hair splayed over the pillow he used every night, sent his hormones into overdrive and his imagination straight into the gutter.

Yeah, Josie Lyons was going to be a big pain in the—libido. He perched on the end of the bed, feet firmly on the floor, his body twisted enough so his back rested lightly against the footboard.

"Seriously? Aren't you going to get comfortable?" She raised up on her elbows and blinked at him.

"I'm fine here. I need to stay alert. It's been a long day. I've been up since five a.m. If I get comfortable, I'll probably doze off. Not a good idea right now."

"But we don't know who these guys are. Or when they'll come

here. Or if they'll come at all. You can't stay awake for days. You have to rest. It's too much." Her voice quivered.

Damn. *Don't get hysterical.* If there was one thing he couldn't stand, it was a crying woman. He had no idea how to deal with them. He despised the resulting incompetent feeling. He shifted slightly, leaning back and lifting one leg onto the bed. She was trying to be strong. In the dim light spilling from behind the ensuite door she'd left ajar, he could make out her expression. Her smile was weak and watery.

"Go to sleep, Josie. I'll watch over you. If I leave, I'll only be gone long enough for a quick reconnoiter. I'll check things out and come right back."

She nodded and cuddled deeper under the blankets. She closed her eyes and wiggled about. Eventually, she stilled. Good, maybe she'd fall asleep. The blankets over her trembled then stilled. A moment later, they shook again. Dammit. She was crying. If she kept quiet, he could ignore it, pretend he didn't notice. Then it came. A muffled sob. She didn't want him to hear. Damn her. That made it worse. Based on what his sister had told him after being trapped in an overturned truck on a freezing cold fall night, delayed emotions were taking over. Like Emily had tried to do, Josie was protecting him from her overwhelming emotions. He knew damn well that unless she released them, she'd never sleep.

"Josie? Are you okay?" It was hard to inject compassion into his voice. It wasn't that he didn't feel it; it was that his urge to cut and run was overwhelming. He'd never been good with public displays of emotion. Hell, even the sight of his parents kissing made him crazy, and he'd been witness to that for thirty-four years. Damn!

"Fine." Her voice quavered.

Oh great. When a woman said she was fine, she was anything but. He hopped off the bed and moved closer. He perched on the mattress beside her and awkwardly patted her back.

She flung the covers to her waist, bolted upright, wrapped her arms around him, and buried her face in his neck. Her tears soaked through the cotton of his shirt. Damn, this was bad. He gripped her arms to push her away. They were silky, firm and warm under his calloused hands. Instead of pushing her away, his arms slid around her, drawing her closer.

He murmured nonsensical words of comfort, like a mother comforting an inconsolable child. Only he felt nothing parental. He suddenly felt like a superhero, the one man who could help her, could calm her and make it better. Yup, he was screwed. Screwed, blued, and tattooed as his grandfather used to say. The expression had never made sense to Gabe, but it sure seemed to fit this awkward situation.

Her body shuddered and quaked in his arms, but she didn't utter another sound. Her obvious attempt to be strong only made it worse. Her strength attracted him, and the feel of her body under his hands? Delightful.

His cock stirred.

Hell no! He would not let his little head overrule the logic of his brain. Not in this lifetime. He was a trained soldier for Pete's sake. He knew better. He'd taken classes on this, on dealing with the emotions of others and how to keep strangers from using them against him. Enemies came in many shapes and sizes.

And this one fit perfectly in his embrace. Josie wasn't the enemy, but he had to distance himself now, or he'd be useless at protecting her and keeping track of their situation. Gradually, she stilled in his arms. She turned her head toward him. Her lips grazed his neck. He might as well have been struck by a bullet. The soft touch jerked through him, tearing him apart.

She leaned back and looked at him. "Make love to me, Gabe. Help me forget all this craziness, if only for a few minutes."

"No." The single syllable was the hardest sentence he'd ever mustered. The word was barely out when her lips pressed against his. Firm, soft, insistent and delicious. "Josie, no." He tried again to convince her.

She wiggled closer, grinding her breasts against his chest. His breath shuddered out.

"I hardly know you, Josie. It wouldn't be making love. It would be sex." The harsh words didn't seem to penetrate her desperation. He would not take advantage of a distraught, overly emotional woman. He. Would. Not.

"Fine then." She nibbled her way up his neck, soothing each tiny bite with a flick of her tongue and a kiss. "Have sex with me."

"This is emotions talking, and maybe the wine. It's not real. In the morning, you'll be fine. Lie back down. Get some sleep." God, he hoped she listened to reason.

"You don't want me?"

Again with the damned quiver in her voice. "I didn't say that. I said you're overly emotional. You'll regret this in the morning."

"I won't. I need this. I need you." She climbed out from under the covers and straddled his lap, wrapping her legs around him. In one quick motion, her T-shirt joined her shorts on the floor, and she thrust her breasts into his face.

He wouldn't do this. He shouldn't do this.

He was *not* going to do this.

He tipped her head up and brushed her lips with his. Yeah, he was going to do this. A man only had so much willpower.

CHAPTER 7

Something sharp scraped Josie's thigh as she rolled over. Every muscle groaned and complained at the motion. She ached like she'd been hit by a car. Reality slammed into her. Yesterday had been the worst day of her life. She groaned and covered her eyes with her hands, blocking the single shaft of sunlight that peeked through a crack in the curtains. Stretching one muscle at a time, careful not to strain anything, she worked the kinks out of her abused body. Crumbs dug into her legs. Why were there crumbs in the bed?

Oh yeah.

After they'd made love, Gabe brought a snack of toast and cheese to bed. She'd kissed him again, and the plate had ended up under them. What had she been thinking? Seducing a stranger? Mortification slammed through her, knocking away her breath. Crap in a hat! She'd seduced, hell, she'd practically raped the man who rescued her yesterday.

She heard whistling from the kitchen. Now she'd have to face him in the light of day. She hadn't done anything this stupid since her cousin had talked her into skinny dipping with a bunch of classmates in high school. Random sex for Josie Lyons was unheard of. Impulsive behavior was equally rare. She was a planner and a firm believer in establishing a solid relationship before introducing sex into the mix. Well, she'd certainly blown those ideals to the heavens last night, and it had been heaven.

She scrambled out of the bed and hurried into the bathroom after locking the bedroom door. Dear God, she was naked! Pushing mortification aside, she washed up, combed her hair, and brushed her teeth. She slipped into his T-shirt and her bra and panties. She threw on the sweatshirt from yesterday and rifled through his drawers until she found socks and sweatpants. She ignored the twinge of guilt about going through his things, but, considering her wonton behaviour last night, what was a little snooping if it was for a good cause? And protecting her modesty was the best possible reason.

"Protecting my modesty?" She laughed at herself. "A little late for that." She brushed the crumbs from the bed into a small garbage can. The dishes from last night's snack were nowhere in evidence. Gabe must have taken them when he got up. She made the bed and paced the room, trying to drum up the courage to face him in the harsh light of day. Eventually, the sound of male voices and the heavenly scent of fresh coffee drew her from the bedroom. Maybe, with someone else present, their first encounter after a glorious night of lovemaking might be less awkward, and that would be a good thing. She could barely look at herself in the mirror let alone face Gabe. Sometimes she was an idiot. Mentally fortifying herself, she entered the kitchen.

"Morning."

Gabe and Dev turned toward her in unison.

"Morning, sleepyhead," Dev teased. "It's nearly nine, and you're just getting up? Late night?"

She blinked at him stupidly. "Um. Yeah. It took me a long time to unwind and fall asleep. I never would have managed without Gabe. He found me some wine." She laughed woodenly. "Seriously, though, it was a rough evening. And I can tell you I never want another day like yesterday. Did you find out anything, Dev?"

"Good morning." Gabe's greeting drew her attention to him.

"Morning." It took everything she had to force herself to look at him and not blush. "Did you sleep well?" Glory be, what a stupid question. He hadn't gotten any more sleep than she had, probably less since he was 'watching' her and keeping her safe. He'd left her several times to check the house and yard.

"Off and on. I had a lot on my mind last night." He looked her up and down and quirked one eyebrow.

Okay, maybe the addition of his sweats and socks had been a mistake that called attention to her attempts to hide rather than making him keep his distance. She refused to look away. Dang. He was handsome this morning, his hair still damp from a shower, jeans slung low on his hips, tight T-shirt defining every muscle in his chest and arms. For a moment, she'd almost sworn she could count the ripples in his abs, the ones she'd traced with her tongue last night.

"Is there coffee?" Her voice was a squeak. She cleared her throat and tried again. "Please?"

"Not much of a morning person, are you?" Dev teased.

"What? Oh. No. I mean, usually I am. I'm a little off my game today." Her voice was hoarse and squeaking all at once. She shrugged and slid into a seat at the table across from Devlin.

Gabe set a cup of coffee in front of her.

"Thanks." She sipped the scalding beverage carefully, searching for balance. Half a cup later, she looked up from her drink. "What did you learn, Dev?"

"I had your pursuer's SUV towed to the impound, and we got some prints off it. It's a rental, but the prints came back to a guy in the system. Are you familiar with Justin Ambrose? He was in the news a lot about five years ago."

"Not that I recall."

"Ambrose went to jail after being convicted of second-degree murder in Chicago. He killed his wife and brother, who were alleged to be having an affair."

His words made sense but the implication didn't. What did this have to do with her?

"Mikah Smith, also known as Mikah Fetisov, witnessed Ambrose running them down with his car. Not only did he hit them, he backed up to make sure he killed them. Smith was put in the witness protection program. Ambrose has some unsavory friends, and the feds thought it best to relocate Smith after the trial. Ambrose was released from prison for good behavior after serving only ten years of a sixteen-year sentence."

"Oh-my-God!" It was unbelievable. This man had hunted down Mikah and killed him for witnessing a hit and run. She'd seen Mikah get killed, and now this murderer was after her. Un-freaking-believable. What crappy luck.

"It's conceivable Ambrose took a couple years to find Fetisov, and when he took him out, you were there. I'm certain your newspaper interview led Ambrose straight to you."

"What a shit-ass series of events. It's almost unbelievable." Gabe paced the kitchen.

Josie was tempted to join him. Her feet twitched under the table, and she had a white-knuckle grip on her coffee cup to still her shaking hands. What were the odds of this happening to anyone, let alone a small-town librarian? She shuddered. Now what? Did she just live in fear until they found him? Or would he think she'd be scared enough to keep her mouth shut?

"He'll keep coming." Dev leaned back and drained his coffee. "Guys like this don't quit. We have three other sets of prints from the car and evidence of at least four different firearms from the rounds in the quarry. When we find him, and we will, he won't escape. He's done this twice before. He'll get life this time."

Life? Big friggin' deal. This was her life they were talking about. Her life and her job, not to mention her sanity. This guy, Ambrose, knew who she was and had a good idea where to find her. She couldn't go home. She had no job. She didn't want to rely on friends and her family was a thousand miles away.

"You can stay here until he's found," Gabe offered.

"That's a good plan."

Josie raised her head to discover them staring at her.

"You okay with that?" Gabe asked.

"Do I have a choice?" She didn't want to stay here. She wanted to go home. She wanted to go to the library and lose herself in stacks of books with happy endings. Staying here with the embarrassment and temptation of Gabe was out of the question. And yet, it seemed she had no other choice. He was a rancher now, but not that long ago, he had been trained by the military, and Dev trusted him. "Fine."

"Don't sound so thrilled," Gabe drawled.

"Well, I'd take off and never be seen here again if I could, but somebody cleaned out my bank account, and I got fired for no reason. I have no money and no place to go. What other options do I have?" God, she hated this. She'd been independent since she was eighteen. Now, she was stuck hiding behind a cop and a rancher. The frustration defied description.

"What do you mean cleaned out your bank account?"

"I went to the bank three days ago to withdraw some cash and there was nothing there. My investments, my checking account, my savings, all gone. The bank is *investigating* it, but they insist I made the withdrawals; which I did not. Then my jerk boss fired me because he couldn't afford to keep me on, and the library had just received an enormous anonymous grant. I don't know what I did to piss him off, but he canned me anyway. I'm penniless, jobless, and if I don't find money for rent by Monday, homeless. I don't have any clothing."

The urge to crawl into a hole was almost unbearable. But she was stronger than that. She'd fight this, fight Ambrose with everything she had. She'd win, or she'd die trying.

"That's entirely too coincidental for it to be random." Gabe refilled her mug and popped some bread in the toaster.

"Ya think?" She immediately regretted snapping at him. None of this was his fault. He was her savior; he deserved better than her shrewish lack of gratitude, and he certainly hadn't deserved her attacking him last night, even if he hadn't fought her advances very hard. "Sorry, you don't deserve that."

"No worries." He slid a plate of toast and jam in front of her. "Eat something. It'll help." He turned to Dev. "So, what's the plan?"

"There's no sign of your assailants in town. They didn't register at any of the hotels or bed and breakfasts. I suspect this was to be an in-and-out job. They'll probably steal new transportation. Stolen vehicle reports will tip us off, if they're still around. We'll leave Josie with you. You carry on ranching as you always do, after you tell your guys what's up. Josie stays here, out of sight. They'll be searching town for her. I'll place my men in the woods nearby. When they come in, we'll catch them before any damage is done. In the meantime, I'll pay a visit to the bank and to your boss and see what I can uncover."

"You make it sound so easy." She sighed.

"Anything but easy." Dev's expression was grim. "I'm just hoping it's short and sweet. Once everything is in place, I'll go to your apartment and bring you some clothing. If they have someone watching the place, they'll put a tail on me. That'll speed things along. All you have to do is stay out of sight and trust us."

So, she was bait. That didn't sit well. Dev had everything lined up neat and tidy. It seemed so simple. Weren't sting operations supposed to be complicated? How could something so straight forward even work? Surely, this Ambrose guy was too smart to fall into an obvious trap.

After a brief discussion of details, Dev departed, leaving Josie and Gabe alone in the kitchen, staring awkwardly at anything but each other.

"Thanks for the toast and coffee," she blurted at last.

He looked at her, his expression unreadable. She wanted the ground to open up and swallow her. This was her first awkward, morning-after conversation. After what she'd done last night, she had no idea where to begin this conversation. Several glib lines from bad movies rolled through her mind. Glib wasn't who she was. Casual sex wasn't, either, but that hadn't stopped her last night.

"Um. Er. Can we just forget about last night?" She stared at the table.

"Can you at least do me the courtesy of looking at me when you're discarding me like yesterday's trash?"

Was that hurt in his voice? She looked at him. Deep furrows of discontent scrunched up his brows, and his lips turned downward. He didn't sound angry, just—disappointed. How could he be disappointed? Didn't all men want the quick, casual fling? No strings? No questions or problems?

"I'm not discarding you." It was the only thing she could think of. "I just don't want you to think I do that kind of thing on a regular basis."

"What kind of thing?"

Heat flooded her face. She jerked out of her chair, knocking it back to wobble alarmingly before she clamped a steadying hand on it. He wasn't going to make this easy on her.

"I don't sleep around. I don't seduce people I don't know. I don't know what came over me last night. I just…" She was unable to construct coherent sentences or half-reasonable arguments.

"Did I say I thought you did?" He leaned back against the counter, ankles crossed, arms folded over his chest. The set of his jaw and bulged biceps belied his calm.

"I just don't think it should happen again. It was a reaction to the stress."

"I tried to stop you," he reminded her.

"Not very hard," she snapped, pacing past him.

"Right. Do you know a man, even one, who would reject a beautiful woman who throws herself at him? Men are easy. Sure, we pretend to have lofty morals and values, but frankly, we're little better than alley cats. I told you yesterday I was attracted to you the first time I saw you. Then the next thing I know, you're virtually naked with your legs wrapped around my waist and your breasts stuck in my face. How is any living, breathing man supposed to resist that kind of temptation? I tried to stop you. I swear to God I tried. But you were insistent, and I'm weak."

"Alley cat? Wow, so flattering."

His argument was confusing at best. He was attracted to her? Any man would do her? It was like he was trying to take the blame while simultaneously blaming her. It didn't work like that. It took two to tango. Sure, she'd taken the lead in the horizontal mamba, but he'd fallen in line without complaint. Okay, maybe one small complaint. The first time. The next three times had been mutual. More than mutual. They'd been ravenous for each other, situation be damned.

She was still ravenous for him, and the current circumstances had nothing to do with it. Sex with Gabe Gatlin was the best she'd ever had. That told her something. You didn't have the greatest sex of your life with a stranger. There had to be a connection for it to be that fabulous.

"Look, Gabe. I'm not brushing you off." She turned to face him.

His scowl made her want to chuckle, and she had no idea why.

"Okay, I am giving you the brush off. But sex with you was

pretty damned good. Okay, it was fabulous. But this isn't the time or place for that. We have to let it go, move on, and focus on getting out of this messed-up situation alive."

"Fabulous?" He smirked, and that delicious dimple in his left cheek appeared to taunt her. "Yeah, it was pretty fabulous," he agreed.

"This isn't a joke, Gabe." She turned around at the end of the room and paced back again.

He snagged her by the arm as she went by.

"Let go of me."

His hand was warm and gentle. She could have pulled away if she wanted to. He wouldn't hurt her. If she resisted, he'd let her go. She froze in place, staring straight ahead at the sunflower clock on the far wall.

"Josie, look at me. Last night was incredible. But it was a mistake. Don't misunderstand me. I don't regret it. But the timing is messed up and all wrong. But, mark my words, we'll be revisiting my bedroom, together, as soon as this debacle is straightened up. We'll be making love again, but not until we know each other better."

Her mouth dropped open, and she turned to stare at him.

From rutting alley cats to making love? In five minutes, this conversation had taken so many twists she was lost and disoriented. She needed a road map to extract herself from this discussion.

"Close your mouth." He pressed gently on her chin.

She snapped her mouth shut but didn't take her gaze off him.

"Making love was inevitable." He smiled at her. "The timing sucked is all. Now, I'd like to kiss you, if you let me. I promise you, we'll both enjoy it."

He leaned in a fraction of an inch. Her gaze went to his mouth. He'd shaved. Last night's five-o'clock shadow had vanished. Kissing him wouldn't leave her red-faced. She should step back and deny him. But dang it all, she wanted to kiss him again and again.

She leaned toward him, tilting her head up and left for greater access. Her gaze found his, and she read the smile there, the arrogant, masculine, sexy smile. He didn't move in. He left her hanging, waiting, until she couldn't stand it for another second. Slowly, she rose to her tiptoes and pressed her lips against his.

CHAPTER 8

Three interminable days passed. Josie was going stir crazy stuck in the house. Gabe had the freedom to come and go. He escaped outside for a reconnoiter half a dozen times every day. The only sign of Ambrose or anyone unknown being nearby was frantic barking by Gabe's dogs on the second day. They'd barked up a storm and then gone silent after scaring the strangers off.

Gabe had brought the dogs into the house to meet her and given them a command to protect. Well trained Australian Shepherds, they'd guard her life. He didn't let them visit long. They were working dogs, not pets.

Josie was going stir crazy. She'd been begging to go outside, even if it was only onto the front porch for a breath of fresh air. Gabe had been steadfast in his refusal to let her outdoors.

He'd been equally adamant they not make love again. Part of her mind acknowledged that what they'd done had been sex, plain and simple. But she was quickly growing to care for Gabe. He had a kind, patient way about him, and when he made a vow, he stuck to it, no matter how hard she tried to convince him otherwise.

He'd made three vows to her since he pulled her off the cliff. To keep her safe, to keep her inside, and to delay making love until her pursuers had been captured. She was okay with the first, but the second two were driving her stir crazy. She might be able to fight her attraction to him if she could get outside and blow off some steam, but he wouldn't even let her near the windows.

The front door opened and banged shut. Gabe stood there smiling at her. She let her gaze take him in. From the tip of his head to the dusty tooled cowboy boots on his feet. His tan Stetson tipped back, exposing his eyes. His button-front western shirt clung damply to his chest; he must have been working hard. Danged if he wasn't the most kissable man she'd ever seen.

"I have to go check on a mare in the barn. Do you want to join me?"

"What's the catch?" She lay on her back on the floor of the living room, looking at him. "You won't even let me peek outside."

"I talked to Dev. He said you can go from the house to the barn and back. I've had the guys make sure nobody was around and, except for the two deer we saw on camera yesterday, we're alone. So, get off your lazy butt, and we'll go check my mare."

She scrambled to her feet and barrelled across the room. With a quick jump, she wrapped her legs around his waist, confident he'd catch her.

He stumbled, but he grabbed her backside and pulled her close for a quick kiss. "Take it easy. It's just a fast in and out to the barn."

"In and out?" She winked at him.

"Not like that." He set her on the ground and smacked her lightly on the backside. "You can try on the boots my sister Emily keeps here. Maybe they'll fit." He opened the closet and extracted a pair of pink and navy cowboy boots from the top row.

"Holy crap. How many pairs of boots are there?" She gaped at him.

"This is nothing. Three rows here and boxes of too-small boots, from toddler to adult, in the basement. You should see our Stetson collection. Nothing goes to waste on a ranch."

His sister's boots didn't fit Josie. They were two sizes too large. For the sake of getting out, even for a minute, Josie was prepared to make do rather than wait for Gabe to find the right size.

When she was outfitted in boots and a warm flannel jacket, he paused with his hand on the doorknob. "You have to promise to listen to me. No kissing. No distracting me. Keep your eyes open, and tell me if you see anyone. But, most of all, promise you'll do everything I say, without question. If I say run, you hightail it out of there as fast as you can go. Straight back to the house. Get inside, lock the door, and hide in the cold storage room in the basement. Got it?"

She saluted. "Aye, aye, captain."

"This isn't a joke, Josie. I'm dead serious, and if you don't promise, you're not setting a single toe outside this door."

"I'll listen. I promise. No shenanigans. Just please, let me outside. I'll stay close, right beside you." She grasped his free hand between hers. "Please, let's go."

After another stern look, he led her outside, locked the door behind them, and handed her the single key. He took off at a rapid pace toward the traditional barn across the yard. She jogged to keep up with his long, hurried gait. She didn't complain about the enormous boots chaffing her heels. The sun felt wonderful on her face, and she knew he was attempting to keep her out of the line of fire. Safety first and all that. Half a minute later, he was closing the barn's man-door behind them and barring it shut. It took several moments of fast blinking for her eyes to adjust to the dim lighting.

Slowly, things came into focus. The center of the barn held a tractor, torn apart, parts strewn all over. A tall, thin man was bent over it. She tugged on Gabe's hand and pointed toward the man.

"That's Jake."

Jake looked up at the sound of his name, nodded, and returned to work.

"I've got my hands working four hours on and four hours off. They keep watch while they do chores. At night, they just patrol the yard. What they choose to do on their off hours is up to them. Most of them sleep, but Jake doesn't sleep much. So, instead, he's working on the tractor. Don't let his casual attitude fool you. He knew we were here before the door opened."

Stalls lined either side of the enormous barn, and a huge labyrinth of pipe walls filled the center. "What's that?"

"Birthing pen. Sometimes a cow needs extra attention, and we bring her inside. Typically, we don't need to, but it's good to be prepared. That room in the back is the tack room. When I teach you to ride, you'll find everything you need in there."

"Yeah, so not happening. I'm not getting on one of those enormous beasts." She gestured toward an occupied stall; most of the others were empty. "Where are all the horses? You said you have a dozen."

"City slicker," he teased. "Outside, at pasture. They don't live in the barn. What kind of life would that be?"

Josie looked around. Despite the row of plexiglass windows high up on the walls and surrounding the entire structure, the barn was dimly lit, except where Jake was working under a bright overhanging light. "Good point. Outside would definitely be better."

He flipped some switches, and light flooded the barn.

"Come over here. This is Misty. She's due anytime now." He ambled to the front of a stall housing a solid brown and white horse with pretty brown eyes.

"She's lovely."

"Come, let her smell you, and you can pet her."

Josie stepped back, hiding her hands behind her back. "I've never been near a horse before the other day. I think I'll just watch. Thanks."

"As a rancher's girl, you have to learn to care for horses and livestock." He ran his hands down the mare's neck in long slow strokes.

For a moment, Josie was jealous of the horse until his words registered. "Is that what I am? A rancher's girl?"

Gabe pulled her to his side and slung his arm around her shoulders. "Not just any rancher. This rancher. And yeah, it's starting to feel like you're my girl."

Misty snorted her disagreement, and Josie laughed.

"Go ahead, look around. Don't open any stalls with horses inside and don't leave the building. I'm going to give Misty a quick check and a brushing." He slipped into the stall, closing the gate behind him. He grabbed a large stiff-bristled brush from a stainless-steel bucket hanging on a nail outside the stall and started brushing Misty.

Josie watched for a while. Listening to his soft soothing voice as he chatted away to the horse about food and ranch life was like listening to him talk to a person, to a friend. His hands were gentle and firm as he worked on the patient horse. He was good with the animal. She'd noticed that before, when he dealt with the dogs. They listened to his commands as if they understood every word. And they must, because they carried out his orders to perfection. Good behavior was rewarded with a pat or some playtime, bad behavior with a stern reprimand. They would, he told her repeatedly, guard her with their lives. Right now, they stood guard outside the barn.

She wandered along the row of stalls, peeking inside each one. They were spotless. No sign of manure and any remaining straw was clean. The feed bins were empty, as were the watering troughs. Clearly, Gabe was a man who liked everything in its place. She wondered how he felt about her coming in and messing up the operation of his ranch. He hadn't complained, but it must bother his innate sense of organization. He got up at six every morning. He came out, worked with the animals, and was back inside for break-fast and coffee by eight fifteen. Lunch was at twelve thirty and supper at six.

He spent hours with Josie, playing cards or watching television. It didn't seem to bother him, but occasionally, he seemed fidgety and antsy. Despite that, he stuck to her like glue and kept a close eye on the goings on of the ranch.

Several times, his phone had beeped, and he'd dropped what he was doing to check on the feeds from the game cameras. They'd seen white tail and mule deer and even a moose. She loved watching the animals. It was peaceful and beautiful. Gabe seemed to share her joy, once he knew it wasn't a human setting off the cameras.

A cat meowed at the end of the walkway. In the second to last stall at the end of the aisle, she found a calico cat resting inside a large wooden crate. The box was four feet square and a foot high. Slowly, she opened the swinging door and inched inside the stall. The cat looked up and meowed softly.

"Hi, precious." Josie moved closer, squatting down to get a better look. Inside the crate, a pile of squirming kittens wiggled beside their mama. Josie held out her hand, fingers curled under like her grandfather had taught her, and let the cat smell her. The cat licked her once and turned her attention to grooming a miniscule black kitten. After a moment, Josie touched the mama gently on the head, smoothing her silky fur. When no objection was forthcoming, she reached slowly toward the kittens. With gentle, trembling fingers, she stroked each of them in turn before carefully picking one up, watching the mama's reaction to be sure she wasn't in danger of getting scratched.

The sound of Gabe talking to his horse and Jake banging away on the tractor faded into the distance as she cuddled the kitten to her chest, revelling in its soft fur and rhythmic purring. Tension flowed from her, and for the first time in days, she felt herself relaxing.

A pair of boots appeared in her vision, and she clutched the kitten tighter and jerked back against the wall. She looked up when Gabe laughed.

"Well, if it isn't Josie and the Pussycats."

She groaned. "You're the king of bad jokes, you know that, don't you?"

"Yup. The guys always ride me about it. No respect from my staff. And, you're supposed to be keeping your eyes open for danger, silly woman. You never even heard me walk up." His voice was gently chiding and teasing. She knew he wasn't really upset.

"Sorry." She apologized anyway. "I was enjoying Midnight's company." She held the kitten up for his inspection.

He didn't take the kitten. Instead, he settled down beside Josie on the floor and stroked the kitten with one finger. "You're naming my cats? Isn't Midnight for an all-black cat rather lame?"

"What would you call him?"

"Cat."

She wrinkled her nose at him. "And what about Mama Cat?"

"Cat."

"You named your dogs. Why not your cats? I'd name all of them."

"I only have two dogs. There are probably twenty barn cats. This is the only one who is remotely tame. Most of them are wild and fend for themselves. That's how a ranch works. You don't name the livestock or you'll get too attached."

"That's so harsh."

"Butterscotch doesn't think so." He stroked the mama cat on the head.

"You jerk." Josie mock-slapped Gabe's arm. "I thought you didn't name them. You were just jerking me around."

"Yes and no." He chuckled. "Butterscotch is the only cat with a name. Well, and now Midnight, I guess. Don't be naming them all. I can't keep them or I'd be overrun in a matter of weeks. I'm only keeping two, and I'm having them and their mother fixed. It's the only way to keep the population down."

"That's so cold."

"No, that's practical. I have enough spayed and neutered cats around to catch mice. Most of the wild ones have wandered in from someplace else. I let them stay, but they fend for themselves. I don't hurt them, but I do keep them to a reasonable number."

"And the wild ones don't breed?" She didn't want to know what kept them in check, but she had to ask.

"They do. There was a point when I had animal services come in and round up the extras and take them for rehabilitation. It set me back a pretty penny. But I couldn't just shoot them, although some ranchers do. I try and balance generosity and reality. I made a size-able donation to the rehab group to help them out. They do a good thing."

Josie leaned forward and kissed Gabe on the cheek. She couldn't help herself. He was trying to be tough and teach her the reality of ranching, but inside, he was soft and gentle and kind to his animals. "You're a softie, Gabriel Gatlin. A softie."

He chuckled and kissed her back. "Sometimes. But know this, I can be a hard ass if I need to be. Now, it's time to go back inside. And no, Midnight cannot come. He's too young to leave his mother and no pets inside the house. Ranch rules."

She didn't argue. She put the kitten back with her mother and gave each of them a final stroke. Gabe had been generous in bringing her out here, and the kittens had been a lovely bonus. As for pets in the house, she understood there was a line between a working animal and a pet, and if you crossed it, the pet could easily dominate and you'd lose a worker. She'd have to make do with visiting the kittens and the dogs when she had a chance. And if she was ever here without danger chasing her, she'd play with those dogs until they were sick of her. She'd make Gabe join in the fun.

CHAPTER 9

They slept cuddled together in the bed. Josie laughed every night when Gabe warned her he'd only stay if there were no shenanigans. He'd stay with her, but they would not repeat the first night's activities. The way he stated it made her chuckle, but his serious vow not to take advantage touched her. She readily agreed because for all that they'd settled into a smooth, functioning daytime routine, she was still tense and unable to sleep alone. Nightmares woke her several times each night, and Gabe's presence kept her sane.

They'd started the second night with him leaning against a pile of pillows on the footboard. By morning, he was laying beside her, holding her hand, the covers separating them. On nights three and four, he joined her under the covers, fully clothed. Each night, they struggled to keep their distance, but by morning, they were cuddled together.

Last night, they'd dropped all pretense. Gabe kept his sweats on, and Josie slept in his T-shirt, but they went to bed with Josie on her side and Gabe curled up against her back, his arm wrapped around her waist. His last words to her had been, "Good night, Josie. If you try anything, I'm leaving."

She'd known he was serious. She peeked over her shoulder at him and could read the strain lines on his face. He was resting but not fully sleeping, either due to her presence or the threat hounding her. She suspected he slept with one eye open for trouble. So, she kept her hands to herself and simply enjoyed having him beside her through the night.

It was in that dark period, just before dawn, when a soft beep sounded from his phone on the nightstand. Josie bolted upright, grasping the covers to her chest. Gabe was already stepping into his jeans.

"Get dressed," he barked.

This was it, the moment they had been dreading. So far, the game cameras hadn't picked up anything this late at night, but they had tonight. Gabe's reaction told her it wasn't a deer setting them off. She hurried out of bed without question. She shucked Gabe's oversized T-shirt and grabbed one of her own. Jeans and socks followed. Next came her runners and a warm sweater. Thankfully, Dev had delivered clean clothing to her yesterday after their trip to the barn. She did have to admit she'd miss schlepping around in Gabe's sweats. It was comforting to be cuddled up in a sweatshirt that carried his distinctive outdoorsy scent.

She stood, fists clenched, waiting for him to speak again. He studied his phone, flipping from screen to screen without acknowledging her. A silent scream of fear and frustration rose in her throat, and she swallowed it back down.

"Three cameras were triggered. Strangers. It's too dark to tell for sure, but probably Ambrose's men if the mugshots Dev showed us were any indication. I don't see Ambrose, but I know he's out there. I can feel it. Dev's team is tracking them. When they get closer, you're going into the basement until we disarm and disable them." His tone brooked no argument.

She argued anyway. "I don't want to just hide out. I want to help."

He crossed the bedroom in three angry strides and stopped in front of her. His stare was icy and no-nonsense. "Listen to me. You're a librarian. I was a soldier. Dev and his guys are cops. We know how to handle this. You're not prepared for this. Please just listen, and do as I ask."

Did he think she was an idiot?

"Ambrose is a violent repeat offender. He's incapable of mercy, and he'll do anything and everything to avoid prison. Please, Josie, let us protect you. I just found you. I can't—I won't—lose you now." He pulled her into a tight embrace as he spoke.

His words chilled her, but his arms around her pushed back the cold. He was right. She had no idea what to do, how to fight. Reading martial arts books and watching Jason Statham movies didn't cut it. Research was great, but some things you only learned by doing.

"When the time comes, and not a minute before, I'll go into the basement. Until then, what can I do? Besides staying away from windows and doors?" She stepped out of his embrace and gestured toward the remains of his clothing. He was dressed in seconds.

"Wait here while I do a perimeter check of the house. Then, when I tell you to, make coffee. Please."

That last word implied so much more than simple manners or requesting coffee. There was a wealth of tension and emotion. It was a plea for her to listen and stay safe.

"Keep your cell phone on vibrate, keep it with you, and don't open this door or any other door unless you hear my voice or Devlin's. Lock the door behind me." He eased the door open, peeked into the hallway, looked left and right and stepped out, closing the door behind him.

On trembling legs, she hurried to lock the door. She glanced at her watch. Four thirteen in the morning. Her stomach clenched in a tight ball and, for a moment, she thought she might be sick. She swallowed back the nausea and paced. What if something happened to Gabe out there? Or one of Dev's guys? It wouldn't be her fault, but it would feel like it was. How could it not be? These men were here to protect her. They didn't deserve this danger. She didn't, either; all she'd done was report a hit and run accident. Okay, it wasn't an accident, it was murder, but she didn't know that at the time.

Now, her life and Gabe's life were in danger. So many men putting their lives on the line because some damned criminal didn't want to go back to jail after extracting his revenge on the last man who'd sent him there.

God, where was Gabe? Had something happened to him? She hadn't heard anything. No banging, no noise, no gunshots, thank God. But he'd been gone for way too long. Did it take twenty minutes to check out a few locks? What was keeping him? Time was just crawling by.

She checked her watch again. Four fifteen.

What?

Two minutes? It had only been two minutes? It felt like hours. He better come back soon, or the waiting would steal the last of her sanity. It was enough that she was in danger; she couldn't handle having her friends in danger, too. If she got out of this alive, she'd never report another accident. She shook her head to dislodge the irrational thought. Yes, she would. She'd always report another hit and run. It was what decent people did, despite jerks like Ambrose.

Would Gabe never get back? She paced back and forth on shaking knees, massaging her aching stomach. What if something happened to him? She'd only known the man for a few days, and already he'd stolen a piece of her heart. It wasn't love at first sight. She'd decked him the first time she saw him, but it was pretty close to instantaneous. He was kind, generous, protective, and he had a he-man attitude that just wouldn't quit. His concern for her welfare touched something deep inside her. When this crap-storm was over, she wanted to get to know Gabe much, much better. No more watching him from across the café and wishing for the courage to talk to him.

A knock sounded at the door. Her heart raced into overtime beating. Blood thundered in her ears. "Josie, open up. It's me. Gabe."

She chuckled at that. As if she didn't recognize his voice. She opened the door and threw herself into his arms, planting kisses all over his face. "Thank God, you're alive. You were gone so long. I thought you were dead."

He laughed. "Josie, I was gone three minutes, four tops. Get a grip. You can't be losing control of your emotions right now. Later, when this shit is done, you can fall to pieces, but right now, I need every bit of calm you can muster."

"Okay, I'm good." It was a lie, and she was certain he knew it as well as she did, but she was trying to be strong.

He wrapped his arms around her like a warm and comforting vice. She leaned into him, absorbing his strength and calm. He buried his fingers in her tangled hair, tugging gently, bringing her mouth to his. He kissed her breathless before he released her. "Okay, the house is secure. Can you make coffee?" He tapped her lightly on the backside.

"Is that your go-to move now? Slapping my ass?"

"Yup. It's a sign of affection. Now, go, make coffee. And eat something." The last order was thrown at her back as she hurried down the hall.

"You're a Neanderthal." She tossed the words over her shoulder with a laugh. She sobered instantly. This wasn't the time for levity, but his ridiculous, possessive attitude was weirdly adorable.

She peeked into the kitchen, making sure the blinds were shut before she entered. Gabe had already checked everything, but she wanted to be safe. It took half a minute to get the coffee started. She grabbed a pastry from the groceries Dev had delivered with her clothing. She bolted it down quickly. She wasn't hungry. In fact, quite the opposite, but today could be a long day. And the first attack on her had shown just how much food the body needed under stressful conditions. So, she'd pre-feed and get in a bite before crap hit the fan.

"Good idea. Eat while you have a chance."

She whirled around to face him, her arms extended to deflect an attack. "Jeepers. Do you have to sneak up on me? How in the heck do you sneak like a ninja in cowboy boots? It doesn't make sense. You should be thumping around. I should hear you from half a block away."

"Normally, you could. I'm trying not to give my presence away. I can't sneak up on Ambrose if he hears me coming, can I?" He poured two cups of coffee and handed her one. He diluted his with an enormous slop of milk and chugged it down. "I'm heading out to meet Dev. You stay inside, and if you hear anything, anything at all, hit the cold storage room in the basement. Find something to push against the door. Don't rely on the lock."

"And don't come out until I hear your voice? Yeah, I've got it. We've been over this a hundred times in the past four days. I won't forget."

"And keep your phone on vibrate. No sound to give your position away." He planted a swift, hard kiss on her lips and headed outside.

Surprisingly, he didn't remind her to lock the door. She locked it and grabbed her coffee. Nothing to do now but wait. She snuggled into her spot in the living room, praying this went fast. How long would it take for them to corral Ambrose? Minutes, hours? Days? She finished her coffee and set the cup aside. Time crawled by.

One minute. Two. Five. She found herself watching the second hand on her watch to ensure she wasn't losing her mind, but time was still going forward. With each passing second, each tiny tick of the hand, her body tensed tighter, her muscles clenched, and fear rose in her throat, threatening to choke her. She couldn't handle this.

The inaction was making her crazy. She jumped up from her seat, dropping her blanket on the floor, leaving it in a heap.

Careful not to be seen from outside, she checked the windows. Closed and locked. As were the doors. Pacing restlessly, she entered every room on the main floor, checked the windows and scoped out hiding places. Padding softly, but quickly, she hurried up the stairs to the second floor and checked those rooms. The recreation room held only a few chairs, a pool table and a shuffleboard table. Unless she wanted to crawl into the beverage fridge, there was no place to hide in there. Nor was there a hiding place in the guest bathroom.

Two guest rooms held beds and small dressers, but no closets. One had an empty padded bench she could squeeze into if necessary. The last room was a reading room, library combination. Lots of chairs but no hiding places.

Okay, Gabe was right. The best place for her was in the cold storage room in the far corner of the basement. She'd have to travel through the main room, the storage room and around a corner to get to the cold, windowless room. But it was well hidden, and there was a good chance that anyone searching the house might miss it.

Finished with her reconnoiter, and newly familiarized with the house, she scurried down the stairs and paced from room to room. She glanced at her watch again. Seriously? It had only been twenty-five minutes? It felt like hours. Maybe another cup of coffee would help her pass the time.

She wrapped her arms around herself. No more coffee. She was already shaking like a leaf. She was freezing cold and pouring sweat. She wanted to shed her sweater, or maybe add a second one. She floundered, trying to get a grip on her emotions. She wasn't even in any real danger. Yet. But she was spiralling out of control. She could almost hear Gabe's voice telling her to calm down, to take it easy. She'd burn up in a fiery adrenaline rush and have nothing left for when she needed it.

She wandered from room to room, rubbing the sweat from her

palms onto her thighs, clenching and unclenching her fists, tapping her hands together. Pacing and twitching and fidgeting. She straightened pictures on tables and fluffed and re-fluffed throw cushions.

Her mouth was dry. She needed a drink. A glass of water did nothing to curb her thirst; all it did was fill her bladder. She quickly took care of that need and paced back to the kitchen. Maybe juice would help. Did Gabe have juice? He must, his kitchen was stocked with everything else.

And where the hell was he? Why hadn't he texted her?

God, this waiting was screwing with her self-control. She was losing her shit.

A frenzy of barking interrupted the silence.

A gunshot rang out, and she dropped to her knees.

Shouting erupted outside, freezing her in place.

Jesus, someone was shooting? Another shot, this one much louder, echoed through the kitchen. She crawled toward the basement and peered down the stairs. Thank God for open concept stairwells. She could see clear into the basement.

Glass shattered somewhere. Someone must have smashed a window. They were coming in. Rising to her feet, she hurried down the steps in a crouch and, reaching the bottom, jerked upright and rounded the corner into the main room. Half a step into the pitch-black room and she collided with a solid wall of flesh.

Her breath exploded out, someone swore, something slammed into her forehead, and the world turned black.

On Devlin's order, Gabe snuck behind the man creeping toward the house. Drawing on his best roping skills, Gabe snaked out his lasso, whirled it round and dropped it neatly over the man's head and jerked him backward to the ground. The motion jarred the man's rifle from his hands, and it dropped to the ground, discharging as it bounced. The man struggled to free himself, cursing and swearing as Gabe tightened the rope and trussed him up, hog-tied tight.

Dirt exploded from beside Gabe's feet as another shot rang out. Abandoning his captive, Gabe sprinted for the relative protection of the trees he'd been hiding in with Dev.

"Freeze." Dev's voice stopped Gabe in his tracks. "Not you, idiot. Him." Dev gestured in the direction Gabe had come from. "Stop or I'll shoot." The man hurried toward his fallen comrade and struggled with the rope.

Gabe hit the ground, and Devlin fired off a shot, hitting the man in the knee and knocking him down. "They never listen," Dev complained over the sound of the man's agonized screaming. "Okay, you go east. I'll head west. Stick to the tree line. We'll circle the yard. Keep your eyes open for tracks. Two down, two to go."

Unless they brought reinforcements. Gabe kept that thought to himself. Dev knew his business and wouldn't be caught unaware. Moving slowly, careful not to make a sound, Gabe crept through the trees, darting from one to another, doing his best to keep hidden; although hiding was difficult when you had no idea which direction your quarry was coming from. It brought back old combat memories. Hunter and prey all rolled into one, the eternal contest of survival of the quickest.

He hadn't been on many unsuccessful missions, but he'd participated in countless successful ones. The key was working as a team and knowing what your teammates were thinking and what they'd do. Combine that with anticipating your enemy's moves and you'd come out the victor. Thankfully, Gabe was familiar with Dev's techniques.

Gabe inched forward, scanning around him for any sign of motion or any unusual sound. Any noise would be one of Ambrose's men. The forest had gone silent at the sound of the first gunshot. It would be a while before the wildlife was comfortable enough to resume its pre-dawn activity.

What was that? There? He halted mid-step, searching ahead of him. Had he seen a flash of color? Gabe waited patiently. The first to move would be spotted, and he couldn't take the chance that whoever was over there was looking in his direction. On the surface, he was calm, but this was the most important mission he'd ever been on. National security was one thing, but the safety of Josie, the woman he was falling for, was another thing entirely. He wasn't going to lose her before he got to know her.

Ahead of him, a man inched forward, away from Gabe. The man moved slowly and carefully, obviously trained in stealth. Gabe followed, his revolver in hand, timing his steps to match his target's. Soundlessly, he decreased the distance between them. He preferred to attack the man and take him down over shooting him, but he'd shoot if he had to. He was trained for it. It was part of his duty as a civilian contractor to the police. He'd have nightmares later, but that wouldn't stop him. For now, he'd creep up on the man and catch him unaware and take him down.

Thirty feet. Twenty. Ten.

The man paused. Gabe slipped behind a spruce and waited. When he heard quiet footfalls, he peeked out. The man was good, but he wasn't perfect. Each step let Gabe know where he was. He'd increased the distance between them, and Gabe had to hurry to catch up. Fifteen feet. Ten. Five.

Gabe leaped on the man's back, knocking him to the ground. The man's forehead slammed into a root, and he went still. Knowing it could be a trick, Gabe waited until he was sure the man was out cold before easing his grip. He tossed the man's semi-automatic rifle out of reach, slapped some handcuffs on him, and rolled him onto his back. Damn. It wasn't Ambrose. Three men down and still no sign of Ambrose. Was he here or had he sent his guys to do his dirty work alone?

Gabe called Dev on the radio and filled him in.

"I'll send Jake to watch him. He's close to you. But I heard glass breaking a minute ago. I think someone's in the house with Josie." Dev kept the conversation short.

At Gabe's feet, the man groaned and tried to rise. Gabe kicked him in the chest, knocking him back down. Where the hell was Jake? Gabe had to get to Josie before it was too late. With his foot on the man's chest, holding him down, Gabe scanned for Jake.

The two minutes that passed seemed like twenty until Jake came into sight. A hundred ugly scenarios passed through Gabe's mind while he waited. If anything happened to her, he'd kill every one of these men with his bare hands.

Breathless, Jake sprinted up to Gabe. "I've got this one."

Gabe took off toward the house at a dead run.

CHAPTER 11

Dimly, Josie heard the sound of cursing.

What the hell? She opened her eyes, and blinding pain knocked her breath away. She snapped her eyes shut and stayed motionless as memories came rushing back. She was in Gabe's basement. She'd run into someone and been hit. At least, that's what she thought had happened. Her head ached abominably.

She wiggled her fingers and toes. Everything seemed to work, though she'd have new bruises on top of her initial injuries. This was turning out to be one rotten week, unless she counted meeting Gabe.

Gabe.

He'd want her to keep a clear head.

She peeked one eye open. A light was on now, and the biggest man she'd ever seen was rummaging through boxes in the corner. Who? What was he looking for?

He turned back toward her, and Josie snapped her eyes shut before he caught her looking. She'd have to catch him unaware, knock him down, and make a break for it. The rummaging resumed, and she risked another quick look.

She was on the floor in the main room in the basement.

Primarily used for storage, the room was full of boxes and unneeded furniture. Gabe had taken her down there on her second day here, showing her how to find the hidden cold storage room in the back. At one time, the family had used it to store things best left unseen by others. Firearms, ammunition. Even alcohol, at one point in the distant past. Now, Gabe only used it as a root cellar and to store canned goods.

Luckily, her attacker hadn't bothered to tie her up. Maybe all that noise was him looking for something to truss her up with. She better act before he found a rope.

Scanning around, she determined she was on the floor, in front of an old couch. There was a wing chair above her head, three old wooden kitchen chairs beside that. She needed a weapon. Keeping her eyes shut and her body relaxed, she mentally ran over the room's layout. There should be a heavy metal lamp without a shade on the table above her. The next feasible weapon was those kitchen chairs, but she doubted she'd be able to throw one with any accuracy.

It would have to be the lamp.

She'd slam it into him and...

And then what?

Make a break for the storage room and risk him seeing where she went? Race upstairs and outside? No. Gabe had told her to stay inside. And she'd heard those shots earlier. How long ago was that? Minutes? Hours? Hell, she didn't even know how long she'd been out. The pain in her head was receding, but it still hurt like the Dickens.

She needed to focus, to plan her attack to the end. She wouldn't have time to think once he realized she was awake. Okay, hit him. Hopefully knock him out and make a break for upstairs. That might be best. She'd have more options up there than down here.

The rummaging stopped and footsteps came closer, almost soundless on the plush basement carpeting. Something nudged her side. He must have kicked her. Another blow slammed into her side and a groan escaped.

Damn! She didn't want him to know she was awake.

"Get up, bitch. You fucking ruined my life. I was free, and now I'll have to go back to jail if I don't end you. How do you want to die? Fast or slow?" He prodded her again with his foot.

She groaned and rolled onto her side before he decided to kick her again. Her kidneys couldn't withstand too many blows like that.

"Get up."

She struggled to sit, hoping he didn't strike out before she was ready. She'd only get one chance at this. Was the cord wrapped around that lamp? She thought so, but, for the life of her, she couldn't recall.

He grabbed her hair and yanked her to her feet. "I think I'll have a little fun with you before I kill you." He laughed maniacally, and her blood ran cold. He was evil.

She might not make it out of this alive. But with God as her witness, she'd go down fighting and hope Gabe arrived before it was too late. Jerking her head back, she tried to free herself from Ambrose's grip. He pulled back. The sound of hair tearing from her scalp cut through her. She didn't even know losing hair sounded like that. And she sure didn't know it hurt like this. She winced as her knees buckled from the pain.

"Stand up, you stupid cow." He yanked on her hair again. She had no choice but to stand or lose even more hair.

Then it hit her. What was the point of saving her hair if it meant losing her life? She swayed on her feet, feigning a blackout. His hold loosened for a split second. She lunged for the lamp, snatched it up and, with her best little league swing, smashed it into his face.

He staggered back and dropped to his knees, his hands clutching his face. Blood streamed from his nose. In a split second, she knew this was her chance. She hefted the heavy lamp over her head and with every ounce of strength she possessed, slammed it down on the top of his head. It made a sickening crunch. She dropped the lamp. Then, bolting up the stairs, she heard his body slump to the floor.

She flew through the kitchen, fumbled with the dead bolt, exploded outside, and ran smack dab into another man.

Fists flying, she peppered him with punches and tried to knee him in the groin. She'd gotten away from Ambrose. No way in hell would she fall into the hands of one of his goons.

"Josie, stop!"

The command penetrated her fear-induced rage, and she froze for a fraction of a second.

"Stop. It's me."

Gabe!

"Oh my God, oh my God. He's there, downstairs. He attacked me. I hit him with the lamp. I think I killed him." Words exploded from her like rushing water as relief flooded her system. Gabe was here. She was safe.

Devlin and another man raced past them into the house.

"Shh." Gabe drew her close, and he caressed her back. "You're safe now. We have them all."

Her barrage of words stammered to a rambling, stumbling halt. Her body quaked with relief. She was safe. Gabe was safe. Oh! But what if she'd killed Ambrose? Did that make her a murderer? But it was self-defence. Her knees buckled, but Gabe held her upright.

"We've got him." Dev led a bloodied, handcuffed Ambrose from the house.

Ambrose fought and swore and threatened Josie the whole way.

"Shut it," Dev warned. "I've read you your rights. You're going down for this, and for the death of Mikah Fetisov, and for assault with intent to cause bodily harm on Josie Lyons. This time we've got police witnesses. You're going down, and you're never seeing daylight again." Dev chuckled. "You're going to jail knowing a woman knocked your ass out cold."

As he led Ambrose past Josie and Gabe, he paused. "I'll be back in a minute to take statements from both of you. Go inside and take a breather."

Josie's knees wobbled again, and Gabe scooped her into his arms and started toward the house.

"Come on, warrior princess. Let's get you inside, and I'll look at that cut on your forehead. If he wasn't going to jail, I'd kill the bastard for hurting you." He stopped walking and looked at her, his blue-grey eyes tender and kind. "Did he hurt you anywhere else?"

"No. I don't think so. Just some bruises where he kicked me." She kissed Gabe on the cheek. Her heart eased at the concern in his voice. Somehow, his caring made everything better. "I heard breaking glass, ran to the basement to hide and slammed right into him. He must have come in through a basement window. He knocked me out."

"Then how'd you get the best of him?" Gabe nudged the door Dev had left open with his foot.

"That lamp. That big, ugly silver lamp on the end table. I whacked him with it, and when he was bleeding, I pounded it into his skull." She giggled and shuddered, a bit drunk with the adrenaline letdown.

"I'm going to bring that lamp upstairs and give it a place of honor in the living room." Gabe set her down on the kitchen table. "Hang tight, I'll get the first aid kit." He was back in seconds. "I'll have to get a bigger kit if you're going to hang around. You seem to be accident prone."

Slowly and carefully, he cleaned her injuries, kissing each one better as he went. There weren't many, just some yanked-out hair and two cuts on her forehead. Her bruises would fade over time.

An hour later, paperwork completed, they stood on the front porch. There would be a trial eventually, but there was no need to worry about that today. There would also be an investigation into the anonymous donation to the library and whether or not it had anything to do with Josie's abrupt dismissal. Bribes were part of

Ambrose's M.O., and getting her fired might be his responsibility. If that were the case, Ramone Garcia would lose his job and face charges.

"I'm so glad this is over." She leaned into the warm strength of Gabe's chest as they watched Devlin's boys climb into the squad cars with their captives. "Is it awful I'm not upset I got shot the day you rescued me?"

His chuckle rumbled against her chest. "You're not the only one who was shot that day. I was shot through the heart by Cupid's arrow."

She groaned. "That is so bad."

He dropped a quick kiss on the top of her head. "Yeah, it is. But you like it anyway."

They laughed together as the cruisers pulled out of sight.

Josie's cell phone rang. Extracting it from her pocket, she read the display. "Weird, it's Devlin's fiancé, the mayor." She connected the call and put it on speaker. "Hello?"

"Josie, this is Mayor Wildwood. I'm calling to ask you to take over the library until an investigation of Ramone Garcia's actions can be completed."

Josie looked up at Gabe, her brows scrunched together. He shrugged.

"You do know I was fired, right?"

"We do. Devlin Duke has explained the situation to the city council, and after our monthly meeting last night, we have decided to suspend Mr. Garcia and re-instate you. As the most experienced librarian, you'll be acting head of the library until the investigation is complete. Are you willing to return to your former position and accept the increased responsibilities?"

Josie stammered for a moment before forming a coherent sentence. "Yes, Mayor Wildwood, I am."

"Excellent. Once the dust settles, we'll re-evaluate how the library is run. The council will be expecting a report from you on what changes are required. Until then, take the rest of the week off and be back at work first thing Monday morning."

The conversation was quickly concluded, and Josie slid the phone back into her pocket. "Wow. This might just be the best day ever, despite all the shenanigans." Unable to contain the joy rocketing through her, she laughed.

"Congratulations," Gabe explained, picking her up and swinging her around. He set her on her feet and kissed her until she was breathless. "Now, show me your sexy librarian look, Miss head librarian."

Josie tipped her head to the side and looked at him over her glasses and winked. She laughed giddily and smirked. "I'll expect more of that corniness when you take me on our first date tomorrow night. But don't get your hopes up. I don't put out on the first date."

They both knew that, in this case, she was lying.

"Do you put out now? Before our official first date?" he asked.

She chuckled at the mock pleading in his voice. "Maybe if you beg really nice."

He scooped her into his arms and carried her into the house for the second time that day. With a cowboy-booted heel, he kicked the door shut behind him.

"Pretty please, with sugar on top."

They laughed all the way to the bedroom.

Love the novella you just read?
Your opinion matters.

Review this book on your favorite book site, review site, blog, or your own social media properties, and share your opinion with other readers. Thanks in advance, Katie.

CONTACT KATIE O'CONNOR

Katie loves to hear from her readers.
Feel free to contact her anytime.

Website: https://katieohwrites.com
Email: katieoconnorwrites@gmail.com

Reviews are an author's life blood.
To thank readers generous enough to leave a review, Katie holds a
monthly draw for a free e-book.
To enter, simply email your review link to:
(katieoconnorwrites@gmail.com)
Each month's winner will receive the e-book of their choice from
Katie's publications.

Thank you in advance, Katie.

ABOUT KATIE O'CONNOR

Katie O'Connor lives in Calgary, Alberta, Canada. She married her high school sweetheart and is living her happily ever after. She is the mother of two grown daughters and is extremely proud of her five grand-children. She has two wonderful sons-in-law and a large support network of friends, family and fellow authors.

Katie's career path has been long and twisted, with most of her life devoted to her family. She's been a waitress, chambermaid, cashier, store manager, as well as a lab and x-ray technician. She is an avid quilter and crafter.

She's dabbled in writing since high school because something drives her to create stories. She swears that it's impossible for her NOT to write. Unsatisfied with one genre, Katie writes contemporary romance, erotic romance and erotica. Recently, she's crafted her first cozy mystery with the intention of publishing a cozy mystery series.

She believes in all things magical; including dragons, fairies, UFOs, ghosts, and house pixies. But most of all she believes in love, romance and hope.

Katie likes to make it up as she goes along and dreams of

publishing a mixed genre novel. It is going to be an erotic, shape shifter, vampire, steampunk, sci-fi, murder mystery, adventure, romantic, western, historical, thriller. It will be her biography.

www.ingramcontent.com/pod-product-compliance
Lightning Source LLC
Chambersburg PA
CBHW022109050726
47591CB00002B/735